REVENGE OF THE

ZEDS

THE SOTERION MISSION II

REVENGE OF THE
ZEDS

THE SOTERION MISSION II

STEWART ROSS

First published in 2014 by Curious Fox, an imprint of Capstone Global Library Limited, 7 Pilgrim Street, London, EC4V 6LB – Registered company number: 6695582

www.curious-fox.com

ISBN 978 1 782 02087 5
18 17 16 15 14
10 9 8 7 6 5 4 3 2 1

A CIP catalogue for this book is available from the British Library.

Cover illustrations by KJA-Artists.com

Printed and bound by CPI Group (UK) Ltd

To Evie

Contents

1

The Ravine

"Guilty!" Yash looked slowly round at the eleven raised hands. "As I expected, the verdict of the Majlis is unanimous."

Cyrus was surprised by his friend's confidence. It was as if he had been Emir of Alba for months, not just a day or so.

"Thank you," Yash continued. "You may put your hands down." He turned to face the prisoner. "Konnel Padmar, you are a traitor. For that crime, as you know, there is only one punishment.

"As a traitor you broke the golden rule of our community – you failed to do your duty. Without duty our way of life – the Constant way – can't survive. But you didn't just neglect your duty, Padmar, did you? You committed a far worse crime. You betrayed me and all Constants, in Alba and everywhere else.

"Konnel," Yash went on, advancing slowly towards his former colleague, "you were a woman in whom we all placed absolute trust, and yet you betrayed us in a way that, even now, we find hard to imagine. You betrayed us to a Zed."

Yash was now staring straight at the short, round-faced woman standing motionless before him. "Padmar, you attempted to hand Alba over to Timur, the foulest Zed of all. For that you will be killed today, at sunhigh."

The sentence, delivered with matter-of-fact bluntness, was no shock. The only sound that greeted its announcement was a satisfied grunt from Bahm, the fallen leader's fiercest opponent. When no human being lived beyond their nineteenth year, death was an everyday occurrence. It was unpleasant but unavoidable, like the bouts of dysentery that swept through the mountainside community from time to time.

Two archers escorted Padmar out of the Ghasar, the wooden assembly hall where the trial had taken place, and into the square outside. The Konnels followed in twos and threes, expressing their agreement at the way things had turned out. They left Cyrus standing alone in the corner furthest from the door. He had been too young to join the ruling Majlis back home and the meeting had fascinated him. Now it was over, he thought again about his decision to lead the vital mission from Della Tallis to Alba, and how it had changed his life. On that long and perilous journey he had learned the basics of reading and writing. His literacy, now the Soterion vault was open, gave him awesome power and importance. It was why Yash had invited him to the trial – the Emir didn't want to fall out with the only person able to reveal the Soterion's secrets. Not yet, anyway.

Padmar had admitted everything. Yes, she confessed with painful honesty, she had indeed fallen for Timur, the fiendishly clever Malik of the Grozny Zeds who had wheedled his way into their community. Glancing briefly towards Cyrus, she acknowledged that her folly had come close to destroying Alba and its precious Soterion. In the process, she had been indirectly responsible not only for the murder of Chima, the previous Emir of Alba, but also of Cyrus' Tallin colleagues, Navid and Taja. Roxanne, the inspiration behind the Soterion Mission, Cyrus' teacher and the noblest, dearest woman he had ever met, had also perished as a result of Padmar's folly.

Cyrus took a deep breath and rubbed his hands over his face. Roxanne's death had left him shouldering an iron yoke of responsibility. Only he had the skills and knowledge to finish the mission. Her exhortation, almost the last thing she had said to him, was carved in his mind as clearly and ineradicably as the inscription on the steel door of the Soterion vault itself: "For my sake and for the sake of everyone, you must go on."

And he would, whatever it took. In a private half-whisper, he repeated the promise he had made as she lay dying. "Yes, Roxy. For everyone, but for you above all – "

"Hey, Cyrus!" Yash's cry echoed through the empty barn. "Come on! Don't stand there muttering to yourself. People will think you're into your Death Month already!"

Cyrus shook his head. "I hope not, Yash. Too much to do before I go! We haven't really started the important bit of the mission yet, have we?"

The newly elected Emir of Alba hurried over and threw an arm round Cyrus' shoulder. "All that can wait, Cy. I need you at my side during the execution. I'm the Emir, but you're the hero!

I can't do anything without you."

As the two men left the Ghasar and walked side by side into the sunlit Square of the Lion, Cyrus wondered why Yash's loud self-assurance made him feel uncomfortable. He had never doubted his own abilities, but he had always tried not to make a show of them. The smaller the dog, his friend Navid used to say, the bigger it tries to make itself. He hoped it didn't apply to Yash.

Executions were rare in Alba, not because of moral objection or squeamishness – after their eighth winter, every Alban, male and female, was taught to fight, and few passed away before they had shed at least some Zed blood. No, their reluctance to take the life of one of their own was purely practical: they needed every able-bodied person alive and fit to help with the vital fighting, farming and breeding that kept the community going.

Officially, the crimes of disobeying a Konnel's orders, cowardice and betrayal all carried the death penalty. In practice, those found guilty of the first two were simply thrown out of Alba and forbidden to return until a full winter had passed. If they survived in Zed-infested territory for twelve moons, they were said to have proved their worth and were allowed to return. But very occasionally – no more than once in every lifetime – a traitor was uncovered. For them there was no alternative but immediate death. The rarity and hideousness of the crime explained the buzz of expectation that shivered through the ranks of the assembled Albans as Yash and Cyrus emerged into the sunlit square.

Konnel Bahm and a pair of archers, anticipating a normal execution, had prepared the communal well standing in the middle of the square. They had unfastened the bucket from the rope and in its place tied a broad noose. The well was preferred to a tree for a very practical reason. If the hanging failed, as sometimes happened, the prisoner was lowered into the water to drown. When this happened, the next ten buckets of well water were thrown away for fear of pollution.

Padmar stood impassive as the archers knotted cords around her hands and feet. Dressed in a simple tunic of grey wool, with her long dark hair tied back and fastened with a wooden stick in the customary Alban manner, she had shed all her former power and majesty. She was just a plump woman with a pale brown face and a small, hawk-like nose. The eyes that not long ago had gleamed black as broken coal were dimmed and unseeing.

Looking her over with a cool detachment, Yash noticed a rust-coloured stain on the ground near her feet. It was Roxanne's blood. It had fallen onto the cobbles two days previously when Timur, realising he was trapped, had thrust a knife into her chest.

Yash paused, looked at the stain and, with narrowing eyes, looked again at the convict. He shook his head. "No, it will not be a well execution, Padmar. I think you should die as your Zed copemate died. By arrows."

It took Cyrus a moment to grasp the Emir's meaning. The Tallin word for an intimate partner was 'wedun' – 'copemate' was new to him. Yash was referring to Padmar's brief but fatal infatuation with Timur, Malik of the Grozny Zeds.

Obeying their Emir's orders, Bahm and his helpers tied

Padmar to one of the posts that held the winding handle over the well. With surprising respect, they adjusted her clothing lest its thickness act as a shield. Meanwhile, Yash had assembled a firing squad of fifteen archers and moved the spectators to one side in case an arrow missed its target and flew off into the crowd.

When all was ready, he reminded his audience, especially the younger ones lined up to his left, why the execution was taking place. "No single person," he said, "not even an Emir, is more important than the community. To betray the community is to betray every one of us, our lives and the principles we have kept alive since the days of the Long Dead. Death is the only possible punishment for someone who has committed such a foul crime."

Later, remembering these noble words, Cyrus would shiver at their dreadful irony.

Yash asked Padmar if she had anything to say. At first she shook her head, apparently reluctant to speak; then, after staring hard at Yash for a moment, she changed her mind. "Yes, Emir, I would like to say a few words," she began in a voice so thin that those standing at the back found it difficult to hear.

"I am sorry for my weakness, and truly sorry for the pain and suffering I've caused. I was seduced, but not so much by a man as by the dream of power. That Soterion, full of the secrets of the Long Dead, is a wonderful, magical thing. We all dream, as our ancestors dreamed, of being able to bring back the marvels of the lost world."

Yash glanced up at the sun and, reckoning it to be at its

highest point, raised a hand for Padmar to stop.

"No, please," she begged, her voice louder now, less tremulous, "let me finish. I have something important to say. Listen, Yash, Konnels and all other Albans! Yes, the Soterion is truly amazing – but beware its power! Cyrus and Roxanne have unlocked a force greater than any of you realise. Take care! Please take care!"

Cyrus glanced around him. The majority of the crowd looked puzzled by what they had heard. The discovery and opening of the Soterion was a dream come true, bringing a real opportunity of better, longer lives for everyone. What possible danger could there be in that?

Nevertheless, on one or two older faces Cyrus noticed looks of concern. Bahm in particular seemed agitated, frowning and twisting his large, gnarled hands. Yes, thought Cyrus, he understands. He's worried by the darker side of what has been discovered: the knowledge and skills waiting to be unlocked will bring enormous power to whoever controls access to them. The despicable Timur saw this and it lured him to his death. Falling under the same spell, Padmar betrayed all she had held most precious. And what now?

Cyrus looked across at Yash. His friend was tutting and shaking his head. "Nonsense!" he said with a dismissive wave. "Too late for excuses, Padmar. Let's get on with it!"

His weasel-faced copemate Sakamir, standing just behind him, nodded in thoughtful agreement.

The execution was quickly done. Yash stepped back, called for silence, raised a hand and, when the archers had steadied their aim, brought it sharply down. All fifteen arrows struck their bare-chested target. A surprised look lit Padmar's eyes and she opened her mouth as if to speak. But no sound came. Her head slumped forward and her hair dropped like a curtain to hide her shame. Moments later she was dead.

The events of the morning left Cyrus feeling wretched. In an effort to clear his thoughts, he took himself off on a solitary walk through the terraced farmland that rose step by step above the settlement. He had not been gone long when he saw a familiar figure bounding down the slope towards him. It was Sammy, the lean and tousle-headed young man the mission had rescued from the Children of Gova on the way to Alba.

"Mister Cyrus, do you reckon I'd make an archer if I got myself trained up?" the lad asked after they had exchanged greetings.

Cyrus smiled. "Of course, Sammy. You'd be a great warrior. Why do you ask?"

"Well, I don't want to be rude or anything, but the Emir, he's gone and rejected me."

"You mean Yash?"

"Yeah." Sammy put out a hand to stroke the enormous dog that had been following a few paces behind him. After the death of Navid, his previous master, Corby had transferred his allegiance unhesitatingly to the young refugee and the pair were already inseparable.

"That's strange," replied Cyrus. "Did he give a reason?"

"Reason?"

"You know, did he say why you couldn't be an archer?"

Sammy pointed to his left eye. The inflammation he had picked up in the desert had gone, but his sight had not returned. "'Cos of this," he said, his lip quivering. "He said you can't 'ave no squinty warrior." He knelt and hugged the dog close to hide his tears.

"He called you 'squinty'?"

"Yeah. An' the others heard it and started calling me that too. It hurt me, that did."

"Come on," said Cyrus, cloaking his anger, "there's no point in moping, not if you want to be an archer. I'll have a word with Yash for you."

Sammy stood up and wiped his face on the sleeve of his tunic. "Thank you, Mister Cyrus. You always was good to me, wasn't you?"

Cyrus laughed. "Don't you start, Sammy. I've already been flattered more than's good for me. Let's go and find Yash and see if we can get him to change his mind. I'm sure he will."

As long as Emir Yash is the same as the archer we first met, Cyrus thought. I really hope he is.

The bodies of dead Constants were burned, a custom from the time of the Long Dead. The reason was no longer clearly understood, but common sense dictated that it was both unhealthy and unpleasant to leave rotting human flesh lying around for long. The only exceptions were the bodies of criminals and Zeds. These were carried outside the walls and thrown into a ravine for wild animals to feed on noisily at night.

If normal custom had been followed, the corpses of both Padmar and Timur would have ended up in the ravine. But Sakamir argued otherwise.

"Padmar was our acting Emir," she said calmly, as if stating the obvious. "And we should treat the body of one of our leaders, whatever they've done, with respect. The murder of Emir Chima and Padmar's business with Timur undermined the position of Emir, weakened it. We need to build it up again, starting now. Make sure the Emir of Alba's respected and obeyed, like they always used to be."

She leaned towards her copemate and ran a hand through his unruly red hair. "You need all the power and authority you can get, don't you my dear?"

Cyrus said nothing. Though he was Yash's chief counsellor, his friend's relationship with his copemate was none of his business. Personally, he doubted the Emir needed further authority. His swift action at the time of the Timur crisis had made him the Majlis' near-unanimous choice. Backed by Sakamir, he had eagerly accepted the post and his confidence was growing by the day.

"I reckon Sakamir's right, don't you Cyrus?" Yash said. "It'd be wrong to leave the body of an Emir to be eaten by wild beasts, even if she was only an acting one."

Cyrus shrugged. "Your choice, Yash. But if you want my advice, I'd suggest burning Timur's body as well."

"What?" retorted Sakamir, arching her thin eyebrows. "A Zed beside an Alban Emir? That'd be a disgrace."

"Agree. Bit of an odd idea, Cyrus. What're you thinking of?"

Cyrus told them what Roxanne had said of Timur's sinister authority. When in captivity, she had seen how his power extended beyond his own Grozny tribe. In the world of the Zeds, Malik Timur had become a legend in his own lifetime. Just the mention of his name brought other barbarians out in a cold sweat.

"So I think it might be best to burn his body," he concluded. "Get rid of him completely. Just in case…"

"In case of what?" snapped Sakamir.

"I'm not exactly sure. It's just I'd feel safer if there were nothing left of him. It's to do with something else Roxanne mentioned. It's weird, but she said the Long Dead believed well-known or important people never died, not completely. Their power carried on after death – they could still make things happen. Sometimes their bodies were somehow stopped from rotting, too."

"Huh! There won't be anything left of Timur's body when the rats have had it," said Sakamir. "Burned or eaten, he'll be gone for ever." Before Cyrus could reply, she added, "Agree, Yash?"

A flicker of embarrassment passed over the Emir's face. "You don't mind, do you Cyrus?" he asked, laying a hand on his friend's arm. "Sakamir obviously feels strongly about this ravine business. But if you really think it's not a good idea, maybe we could find a way …"

This was no time for argument, Cyrus decided. For the mission to succeed, it was vital they all pulled together. "Don't worry, Yash," he said lightly. "Sakamir's probably right – at least, I hope she is!"

To show there were no hard feelings, he gave her a friendly smile. Her lips moved in response, but there was no friendship in those grey, deep-set eyes. Cyrus put this partly down to jealousy. Because he could unlock the secrets of the Long Dead stored in the books of the Soterion, for the time being he was more important than her Emir. She was probably suspicious of him because he was an Outsider, too. He didn't blame her for that – Bahm mistrusted him for the same irrational reason.

Whatever happened, Cyrus told himself, he had to curb his natural impetuosity. Antagonising his hosts would get him nowhere. The Soterion was theirs, after all, and he was in Alba only at their invitation.

After Sakamir had left to arrange how the bodies of Timur and Padmar were to be disposed of, Cyrus asked Yash about Sammy being trained as an archer. To his surprise, the Emir immediately lifted his ban.

"Alright, if you think he'll manage, I agree," he said. His tone sounded relieved. "It wasn't really my decision anyway... So please pass on the good news to him. He's a good lad – a man now, really. That one eye of his is probably sharper than most people's two! I'll apologise to him myself about that 'squinty' business. It was only a joke, Cyrus."

Cyrus thanked him and went to find Sammy. He was relieved to find he'd been wrong about Yash. The Emir was still the same good-hearted friend he had been all along. Pity his copemate was so prickly, though. Thinking over what Yash had said, he was sure it was she who had refused Sammy's wish. He must watch her. Experience had taught him that prickliness could develop into something more than unpleasant.

Late that afternoon, after an armed patrol had carried Timur's corpse outside the walls of Alba and cast it into a ravine some thousand paces distant, Cyrus and Sammy joined the crowd gathered to watch the bodyburn. The near-naked bodies of Navid, Taja, Roxanne and Padmar were carried to the huge fire stone near the Patrol Gate, the lower of the two entrances into Alba. A tall pyre of brushwood and logs had already been erected on top of the flat-topped rock on which corpses were incinerated.

Two ladders ran up the side of the pyre. A couple of strong archers, one at the head, the other at the feet, lifted the bodies and laid them next to each other on the top of the pyramid. When everything was ready, Yash took a flaming brand and lifted it above his head.

"Alba, courage, duty!" he yelled.

With one voice, the crowded responded. "Alba, courage, duty!"

As the sound echoed away, the Emir lowered his brand to the tinder and the summit of the rock was soon blazing like a volcano. The crowd drifted away until just two figures stood arm in arm, gazing into the flames.

"Bit special, wasn't she, Mister Cyrus?" said the younger of the two, his eyes fixed on the fire.

Cyrus let go of Sammy and folded his arms across his chest. During his seventeen winters of life he had witnessed hundreds of fireburns. Most were just routine disposals. He had vague memories of standing sorrowfully beside the pyre on which his parents' bodies had lain; later, he had difficulty holding back tears at the fireburn of Pari, his young wedun who had bled to death shortly after the delivery of their stillborn child.

This one was different, more troubling. Not because it marked the end of wretched Padmar, nor because it reminded him of the deaths of Navid and Taja, painful though they were, but because it brought to mind once again the awesome responsibility he bore. Roxanne's passing had deprived him of that most rare and precious of all gifts – a fellow human being with whom he had merged in both heart and mind. Like two streams meeting, each had flowed into the other. As he watched the thick grey smoke drift up from the fire stone into the darkening sky, he heard again her dying exhortation: "For all our sakes, Cyrus, you must go on. You must go on."

Sammy, having received no answer, said nothing for while. Then, with wisdom remarkable for a young man, he said carefully, "I'm still 'ere, Mister Cyrus. You ain't all alone, you know. There's two of us what's going to carry on the mission."

Cyrus looked at him and smiled. "Thanks, Sammy. Yes, two of us. I almost forgot. It'll be much easier with two."

Four thousand paces away, on the other side of the valley that ran along the sunrise boundary of Alban territory, two Zed minds were also contemplating the future with uncertainty.

"Malik not come back," grunted Jamshid, scratching angrily at his lice-infested groin.

Giv, the younger and brighter of the two Zeds, shook his head. "Timur come back. He tell Giv wait."

His weasel-faced partner snorted and picked at a rabbit bone, all that remained of the day's kill. He cracked it open with his teeth and sucked at the bloody marrow. They had no means to light a fire, and had subsisted on wild fruits and raw meat ever since Timur's departure. A full lunar cycle having elapsed since he had left them on his foray into Alba, they were hungry and bored.

When he had extracted the last of the marrow and wiped the blood dribbling down his stubbled chin, Captain Jamshid stood up. "Jamshid going back to Grozny," he announced.

A look of horror passed across Giv's face. "No, Jamshid, no!" he shouted, leaping to his feet. "Malik come back and ..." He left the sentence unfinished, unable to imagine what terrible things Timur would do if he found they had abandoned him.

Giv's terror reminded his colleague of their leader's unquenchable thirst for inflicting pain. Jamshid had seen and heard its victims too often not to catch the younger man's fear. He scratched himself again, more thoughtfully this time.

"Stay here, soon Constants find us and we die," he mused. "Go back and Malik come, we also die. Worse. Big screaming." He sat down again.

Giv resumed his seat and the two men sat without uttering a word until the shadows lengthened into twilight and the first stars shimmered through the canopy of trees overhead.

"What they?" asked Giv, lying back and pointing up at the pinpoints of light dotting the night sky.

Jamshid looked blank. "What what?"

"Little suns," explained Giv.

"Malik call, er, slars," Jumshid replied, unsure whether he had remembered the word correctly.

"Slars, slars, slars," repeated Giv.

After he had said the word perhaps fifty times, he suddenly stopped. "Slars' light," he muttered slowly. "Giv see in night."

Jamshid looked at him and frowned. "Malik say you ratbrain."

"No, not ratbrain!" Giv got to his feet. "No Constants in night. Giv see in night with slars' light."

"You still ratbrain."

Giv ignored him. "Jamshid stay. Giv go find Malik Timur in night."

Without another word, the young man bounded off into the darkness, leaving Jamshid staring after him in disbelief. "Ratbrain," he muttered as the sound of his partner's footsteps died away. Shortly afterwards he fell asleep and dreamed of Giv with two gleaming slars where his eyes should have been.

Jamshid had the instincts of a wild animal. No matter how tired he was, he woke at the slightest noise. The first light of dawn was breaking through the trees when a rustling in the bushes to his left had him sitting bolt upright and reaching for his rusty gut-ripper. He relaxed and lowered the weapon as the grey shape of Giv emerged out of the thicket.

"Giv back," the young man announced in a hushed, almost wondrous voice.

Jamshid snorted. "Giv back but no Malik. Where is Malik?"

"Malik here," said Giv in the same reverential tones.

The Captain grabbed his gut-ripper and leaped to his feet. "Jamshid still here, Malik," he cried, looking wildly around him.

"Jamshid wait for…"

His voice trailed off into a horrified silence. In his left hand Giv was holding something strange. Swinging gently from side to side, it looked like a massive white club. But it wasn't a club, it was –

"Malik!" howled Jamshid, raising his gut-ripper and charging at Giv. "Giv kill Malik!"

Had the vicious weapon struck home, the blow would have slain Giv in an instant. But the younger man was too agile. Seeing the blow coming, he skipped to one side and swung the object he was carrying hard at his assailant's head. Skull met skull with a loud crack and Jamshid staggered back.

"Listen!" screamed Giv, jumping up and down before his dazed companion. "Giv find Malik body. Constants think they kill Malik. Giv say no."

Jamshid stared in disbelief. "You loony man," he said quietly. "Tell Jamshid – or he kill you."

Slowly, in broken sentences and simple words, Giv told his story. He had followed Timur's path towards Alba and, after walking for a short while, he noticed what appeared to be a fire in the distance. He advanced cautiously towards it until he found himself gazing up at the walls of Alba standing tall and pale in the moonlight. The fire was blazing on the other side and although he couldn't see what was happening, the smell told him immediately what was being burned. All Grozny Zeds recognised the aroma of charred flesh, but for different reasons from Constants.

Giv had blundered around in the dark for a bit, trying to find a way to enter the citadel. He finally gave up and headed back roughly in the direction he had come. Finding a steep-sided ravine in his path, he chose to cross it rather than find a way round. He had scrambled noisily down the steep side and was making his way across the rocky floor when he tripped over something soft and fleshy.

The bottom of the ravine was in shadow and at first Giv couldn't believe his eyes. Undeterred by the stench of putrefaction, he knelt and examined the corpse more closely. The same pearly skin scarred with a Z tattoo on the forehead, the same long white hair… He gingerly pushed open a slimy eyelid. Yes, despite the work of an early maggot, the same red eyes. It was his Malik.

Giv sat back on his heels in disbelief. No, he said to himself. Not happen. What Giv do? What Grozny do? Malik not die, Malik not die, Malik not… The young man's shock and fear were interrupted by a flash of instinctive inspiration. He, the humble Giv, would bring Timur the Terrible back to his people. Not all of him – the corpse was too heavy to carry or drag on his own – just the important bit. Kneeling again, he took out his knife and began the grizzly business of decapitating his master.

When Giv had finished his story, Jamshid sat quietly for a while before saying, "You right, Giv. Timur not dead – Jamshid and Giv have Malik head. Timur Malik live in his head."

Giv considered this for a moment. "Head not speak," he frowned.

"Jamshid will speak Timur words," grinned the Captain.

Giv did not like the implications of this. "No, Giv speak

Timur words."

Jamshid reached for his weapon and growled, "Jamshid has gut-ripper."

Giv cradled the stinking trophy to his chest. "Giv have Malik head," he retorted.

There was another long silence. In the end, they agreed both would act as Timur's voice when the head was safely back with the tribe. The plan was ridiculously optimistic and would certainly have led to bitter squabbles between the two men, and probably to the death of one. Its effectiveness was never put to the test. Long before they reached the Grozny, both Jamshid and Giv and their rotting symbol of authority were taken prisoner. Their captor, had the two ever met, would have been more than a match even for the mighty Timur.

The blow fell early one drizzly evening as they were passing through a patch of scrubby woodland. The path was narrow. Jamshid went first, his gut-ripper hanging idly at his side. Giv, holding Timur's head by its long white hair, followed three paces behind.

Giv, blessed with sharper hearing than the older man, heard it first. To begin with, he thought the noise must be a snake and he checked to see where he was putting his bare feet. There was nothing. The sinister hissing grew louder. Jamshid had now stopped and was peering into the trees. The sound seemed to be coming from every side.

All of a sudden, it ceased. Two dozen figures slipped silently into view and spread out around the startled Grozny. Each gripped a long, metal-tipped spear and was pointing it directly at them.

Giv stared around in open-mouthed amazement. The tattooed warriors surrounding them were clearly Zeds – the same bare feet, scarred, half-naked bodies, unkempt hair and cruel, stupid faces as the men he had been brought up with. But there was one crucial, astounding difference: among their captors there was not a man to be seen.

2

The Soterion

The morning after the fireburn, Cyrus awoke to the sound of rain. For a few moments he lay thinking about what the change in the weather brought. It meant water for the terraces that rose in measured steps above the settlement; it meant replenishment for the great well in the centre of Lion Square; for him personally it meant much more.

The rainy season heralded the onset of his seventeenth winter and his entry into what might well be the last twelve moons of his life. He rubbed his eyes. Twelve moons? He really must start using the language of the Long Dead that Roxanne had taught him. A complete cycle of seasons was a year. He had a little over a year to live – at most.

And there was so much to do! A current of urgent energy surged through him. He rose quickly from his straw mattress, pulled on the leather cape Yash had given him and picked his way between the sleeping Konnels to the door. Before stepping outside, he checked the pouch at his belt. Yes, it was still there. The key to the Soterion, to hope and to the future.

Leaving the dormitory, he turned right for the lower Patrol Gate and the site of the fireburn. He needed to say one final farewell. The flames had died down before the rain began and the sodden ashes – Roxanne's ashes – were being carried off the rock in little grey-black streams. He watched as they hurried down to the waterlogged ground where they gathered in muddy pools before flooding under the gate and out into the woods and wastelands beyond. By the end of the day, all would be washed away. The stone altar, clean and bright, would await its next occupant. As it was with the ashes, he determined, so it must be with the events of the past half-year. However painful, from now on he had to look forward. His past was a mountain from whose summit he could see the future, not a block in the road ahead. He was sure that's how Roxanne would have seen it.

He stood gazing at the scene, then turned and walked rapidly along the course of the wall towards what was already being called the Soterion Gate. The guards recognised him straight away and let him through. Would he need an escort? There might be Zeds...

Cyrus shook his head. "Thanks for the offer, but no need. There's less chance of Zeds being out early on a morning like this than there is of them flying over the walls. I reckon I can take care of myself. Anyway, Asal and Shyad and the other lads are still on guard there, aren't they? I'll yell if I get into trouble, ok?"

The guards waved him through and he set off along the slippery path that wound down the mountainside to the vault.

He met no one on the way and was soon turning the key in the lock of the stainless steel door. As it swung open, he was greeted once again by the wondrous smell of leather and paper and ink and glue. All was as it had been two days earlier when he had lifted the dead body of Roxanne in his arms and carried her out into the sunlight. He swallowed, trying hard to put the memory aside.

"It's over," he muttered to himself, striking sparks to light the torch Yash had tied to an iron ring by the door. "It's over."

Orange-yellow light filled the chamber and, for the first time, he made a careful inspection of its contents. The three sets of shelves, one on each of the walls away from the door, contained perhaps as many as six hundred books. They were divided into sections with labels such as Science, History, Literature, Mathematics, Theology … the words meant little to him.

He moved to the section where he had found Peter Pan, one of the three books by which Roxanne had learned to read. He singled out another volume, took it closer to the light and tried to read. *Tell me, Muse, the story of that resourceful man who was driven to wander far and wide…*

He stopped reading. Though he wasn't sure what 'resourceful' meant, the story could be his. He too had been driven – more or less – to wander far and wide. How weird! He wondered who or what a 'Muse' was. Man or woman? He glanced at the title for a clue. *The Odyssey*. That didn't help. Returning to the story, he found himself tripping over further vocabulary. What was a 'holy citadel'? Roxanne had once tried to explain 'holy' but he still wasn't sure.

Having struggled to the foot of the page, he put the book down on the desk in the centre of the vault. This was no good – at this rate, it'd take him the rest of his life to read just one story. He must leave *The Odyssey* for the time being and find a book that explained words. Surely there was such a thing? The Long Dead must have known not everyone would be able to read fluently, not at first anyway? A word-meaning book would also allow him to understand properly the letter he had come across after Roxanne's death. He was keen to see what it said about the Salvation Project.

He found what he needed quicker than he expected. It was in a section called 'Reference', between 'Encyclopaedia' and 'Thesaurus'. It had Dictionary in gold letters on the blue spine. Once he had opened its covers, he was enthralled.

It was like entering a magic cave in a dream, a Soterion within a Soterion. Old familiar friends were there, lying side by side with strangers. It didn't take him long to get the hang of it. When he had done so, he turned to 'holy' and read, 'perfect in a moral sense'. He understood that, just about – but there was more. 'Pure in heart' – easy enough to grasp. But Ozlam, the High Father of the Children of Gova, had called himself holy – and he certainly hadn't been pure in heart.

Cyrus read on, eagerly eating the delicious words. 'Associated with God or gods...' Still more meanings to look up. And so it went on, word after word, line after line, each leading to another in a wondrous trail of discovery. With every step, he felt as if a door into the world of the Long Dead was being opened just a fraction wider. It was thrilling, mesmerising.

He was so engrossed that he didn't notice he had visitors.

"Hello Cyrus!"

It was Yash, with Sakamir standing just behind him. The flickering torchlight threw uncanny shadows over their faces. "Guards said you were down here. What're you doing?"

Cyrus did his best to explain. He showed them the shelves of books before turning to the table and picking up the letter he had found on first entering the vault. He'd been so lost in the dictionary, he'd forgotten about it.

"Remember me mentioning this?" he asked, carefully picking up the dry, crackling paper and motioning to his friends to sit on the couch. "It helps us understand a lot, though there are bits I don't get. I'll read it out loud once, then go over it again. We can look up the words we don't know in this book." He held out the volume he had been reading when they came in. "It's called a 'dictionary' and it gives the meaning of every word, like –"

"Come on, Cyrus!" interrupted Sakamir. "Yash and I want to know what's on that bit of paper."

He glanced at her sharply but said nothing. Sitting in the chair, he spread the letter out over the desk and began to read.

Greetings –

I imagine you're reading this, whoever you are, because you want to know what this place is all about. I'll try and explain as briefly as I can – I haven't got much time left.

Back in May 2017, an epidemic of what we called the Mini-flu struck the world. Everyone got it but, as the slight symptoms lasted only a few hours, no one took much notice. They should have. The disease was mutating the mechanism in our DNA that controls ageing. The delayed effect kicked in from August 2018.

Before this we had aged slowly, many of us living to 70, 80 or even 100. Not any more. Nowadays everyone suddenly grows old and dies during their 19th year. The speed of change is terrifying – 3-4 weeks at most. We call it the "Death Month".

Adults over 19 went first, billions of them. Services collapsed, power failed, plagues swept the planet, rotting bodies piled in the streets. In a few short months, science, literature and knowledge – thousands of years of human civilisation – disintegrated. Fortunately or not, we were saved from full-scale warfare because governments ordered the destruction of all domestic and military weaponry immediately they saw what was going on.

Less than a year has passed since it all began – and it's mayhem out there. Law and order have broken down and gangs of desperate teenagers terrorise the streets and countryside. I can understand how they feel. They know their 18th birthday is their last: at some point during the next 365 days they'll wake up to find their skin a little tighter and flecks of grey in their hair. They'll be in their Death Month, with just days to live. There are many suicides.

I'm one of the last old-style adults. As my Death Month started about three weeks ago, I reckon I've got only a few hours to go. By the end of July, there won't be a single one of us left.

I guess you understand something of what I'm talking about. Your DNA – if you understand what that is – must be the same as ours. That means you and the people you live with are all 18 or younger. I can't imagine your world, though it must somehow have evolved out of ours – the one you can probably see in ruins all about you.

So, what's this strange depository you've managed to get into? Racing against time, a group of us have tried to secure a tolerable future for our kids. We've set up camps for them to manage on their own when we're gone. Maybe you're from one of these? I hope so.

We've also built this place, a secure vault containing all the human knowledge and wisdom we could gather. It's for you, young stranger – as long as you're able to access it. We've included the data of the Salvation Project, a medical programme aimed at reversing the DNA-altering symptoms of the Mini-flu. The scientists died before their work was finished. I don't know how close they came to success.

I trust you'll be able to use what you find here. It may allow you to pick up the pieces and carry on where we left off. Try and make a better fist of it than we did! With that wish in mind, I've named this vault after an ancient word for salvation: Soterion, the only place of hope in a world looking so desolate that it breaks my dying heart.

Dr Rebekkah Askar
10 July 2019

When he had finished, Cyrus interpreted the bits that made sense to him and looked up the words none of them knew. He told Yash and Sakamir about 'years' and how, when she arrived at Della Tallis, Roxanne said she reckoned they were in the year 2106. Judging by the state of everything remaining from the time of the Long Dead, he thought the date might be an underestimate. But if she was right, it was now 2107 and Askar had written her sad message 88 years ago. He had no idea what 'Dr' meant.

The letter confirmed the truth behind several Constant legends. The Long Dead had indeed lived differently from them, some of them enjoying very long lives. Cyrus was intrigued by the phrase 'human civilisation'. The dictionary definitions were complicated, so he went back to 'civilised'. 'Advanced beyond the primitive savage state,' he read.

"That makes sense, doesn't it? We're what they called civilised, and the Zeds are not."

Yash was not listening. "Cyrus," he said, leaning forward eagerly, "can you read that bit again about military and something that sounded like weapons?"

"This bit you mean? *Governments ordered the destruction of all domestic and military weaponry immediately they saw what was going on.*"

"Yes, that's it. So what's it mean exactly?"

Once Cyrus had explained the difficult words to him, Yash let out a low whistle. "You know what it's saying, don't you?" His eyes were bright with excitement. "They had much better weapons than our bows and swords. Wow! Just think what we could do if we had them!"

He rose and began pacing up and down the room. Watching him, Cyrus remembered Padmar's warning about the Soterion's dark power. Please, Yash, he thought. Not you as well!

With rising excitement, his friend continued, "I'd smash the Zeds and become the most important and powerful –"

"Come on, Yash!" said Sakamir, rising to her feet. She looked annoyed, Cyrus thought, as if her impetuous copemate had said too much. Had the two of them already started planning to use the Soterion's power? No, that was ridiculous. Yash was a good man. He was just a bit carried away by what the future might bring, that was all.

"We can't even read yet," Sakamir went on. "Forget those daft ideas, Yash, and concentrate on the basics." She smiled apologetically at Cyrus. "I'm right, aren't I?" As she was speaking, she moved to stand behind his chair and rested her hand on his shoulder, high up near his collar.

"More or less," he replied. "We can't do much until several of us can read properly." Sakamir's finger was now rubbing the nape of his neck, slowly, almost – but not quite – imperceptibly.

This was ridiculous! Surely Yash could see … unless, of course, this was prearranged and he chose not to notice.

Cyrus stood up abruptly. "Right. I'll start reading as many books as possible – and teaching others to read at the same time."

Sakamir, calm and inscrutable, moved back to her copemate's side. "Perfect, Cyrus. Yash and I will choose the people for you to teach. You can start tomorrow."

So I'm not allowed to select my own pupils, thought Cyrus. Oh Padmar! You weren't stupid, were you? It had once seemed so simple: all Roxanne and he had to do was reach Alba and open the vault… Open the vault? It was beginning to look as they had opened a nest of vipers. Yash was focused on power rather than learning, and his wily copemate seemed prepared to do anything to get what they wanted. He had to be careful, so very careful.

"Yes, Sakamir, I'd be happy to start tomorrow," he answered

cautiously. "The sooner we get other people reading, the better." Irritated by the way she had given him orders, he added in as lighthearted a manner as he could manage, "By the way, don't forget that if I died tomorrow this lot wouldn't be much use to you."

Sakamir arranged her thin face into another joyless smile. "Oh! Don't worry about that, Cyrus! Yash and I'll guard you with our lives, won't we Yash?"

"Of course!" He waved a hand at the shelves of books. "And, er, I've been thinking... It'd be safer if all these were stored in Alba. We can use the Ghasar."

Cyrus frowned. Yes, they had been planning. Once in Alba, the Soterion would be under the personal control of the Emir.

"Probably best to leave them here," he countered. "After all, they've survived in this place pretty well for almost a hundred winters, er, years. It's dry and it's safe." He pointed towards the massive steel door across the vault's entrance. "And no one's going to get through that thing in a hurry."

"Sorry, Cyrus," said Yash firmly, "but I can't agree. Guarding the Soterion would mean taking archers off other duties. What's more, the Zeds'll get to hear of it – yes, I know they will – and then it'd be just about impossible to keep the path between Alba and here open. There'd be Zed ambushes every step of the way, wouldn't there, Sakamir?"

"I'm afraid there would, Cyrus," she replied with a theatrical sigh. "I know how much this place must mean to you, but I think Yash is right. To keep the books safe, we'd better move them into Alba."

Cyrus looked at her, then back at Yash. They had clearly made up their minds and there was no point in arguing. Besides, as the books belonged to Alba, there was nothing he could do about it. Only much later, when it was too late, did he realise he should have resisted the change more fiercely.

"Alright," he said, "but I'd like something in return."

"As you know," answered Sakamir in the same oily tone she had used when promising to protect him with her life, "we are in your debt, dear Cyrus. What can we do for you?"

"I'd like my young friend to be one of those I teach to read," said Cyrus.

Yash nodded. "You mean Sammy?"

"Yes, Sammy. Sakamir?"

"If the Emir agrees," she said, her face an expressionless mask, "I agree."

Quite clearly she did not, though Cyrus was not sure why. It looked as if she wanted to keep him isolated from his close friends and companions. He'd be easier to manipulate like that.

The transfer of the Soterion library to Alba was completed by sundown, as Yash wished. Cyrus positioned himself in the Ghasar to receive the books as they came in and did his best to keep them in their original order. Sammy worked with him, helping to stack the dusty volumes on the floor.

"They going to be alright here, Mister Cyrus?" he asked as he kicked aside a startled cockroach nestling in a crack between the boards.

"I hope so. At least we'll be able to read them without leaving

Alba. Might be safer, too."

"So long as this place don't catch fire… "

The conversation was interrupted by an archer carrying two low piles of books on a sort of shiny metal tray.

"What's that?" asked Cyrus as he handed the contents of the tray to Sammy.

"Dunno, Cyrus. Thought you might. There's five or six of them down there. I brought one up so you could take a look and see what you wanted to do with them."

Cyrus took the object and examined it. It was rectangular, about an adult handspan on the short side and a little over a foot wide, with holes of different sizes along the edges. The whole thing was no more than a fingerjoint thick. He passed it over to his helper.

"What do you make of this, Sammy? Obviously some Long Dead gadget I've never seen before. Have you?"

The young man turned the tray over in his hands. "No, never seen one. But them holes has metal bits sticking up inside. You can see them, all gleaming. And where there's metal, there's that stuff what made the killer fence where I come from."

"You mean electricity," said Cyrus. That was another word he needed to look up. He made a mental note to do so as soon as he had finished arranging the books.

A cry from Sammy interrupted his thoughts. "Wow! Look! It opens up!"

The tray appeared to be in two parts joined by a hinge. On the inside of one half were rows of letters and numbers, and a name. The other was covered with a grey, glassy substance.

Sammy poked it and grinned.

"Bet this was important," he said. "What you goin' to do with it, Mister Cyrus?"

"Well, it's not much use to us until we know what it is. As you say, it probably needs electricity, which we haven't got. Let's concentrate on the books for the moment."

He thanked the archer and asked him and his colleagues to move the books first. If there was time while it was still light, they could bring up any further trays they found.

Sammy looked disappointed. Towards the end of the evening, when the transfer of the library was nearly complete, he went down to the Soterion himself. He wanted to check no tray had been overlooked, he said. He returned with two more, bringing the total in the Ghasar to five. Finally, as night was closing in, Yash looked around the vault to check that it was empty and shut the steel door. After locking it, he kept the key himself. For safety's sake, he declared, henceforward it should remain in the possession of the Emir of Alba.

The Grozny Zeds held women in contempt. They were, in the words of the late Malik Timur, "poisonous flabtoads" whose sole purposes were to provide recreation and maintain a supply of new Grozny warriors. So when Giv and Jumshid found themselves ambushed by a band of women, their first reaction was one of total scorn.

"Breeding slaves!" muttered Jamshid. "Smash them!" He raised his gut-ripper and advanced on the nearest of his would-be assailants. With a slight hiss, she nimbly jumped back a couple of steps. Jamshid followed, and again she retreated.

Before he could react, he felt a sharp stabbing pain in his rump. With a roar, he spun round to confront his assailant. As he did so, a second spear pierced his left side. He squealed in hurt and frustration, and swivelled to face his elusive enemy. Another stab, cry of pain, furious turn – and another and another.

Jamshid was bleeding heavily from seven gashes to the fleshy parts of his body. Frenzied by the goading, he hurled his gut-ripper at the nearest attacker. As she sidestepped the flying weapon, he lumbered towards the gap. A spear shot between his calves, and he tripped and fell. Immediately a swarm of hissing women fell upon him, pinning him spread-eagled to the ground.

Not far off, the same fate had befallen Giv. A warrior stood astride each of the wounded Grozny, a razor-sharp spear poised above their throats.

"Kill?" asked the woman who stood over Giv. She glanced across at a colleague standing slightly apart. Well built, of medium height and carrying the same type of metal-tipped spear as the rest of the warband, she was distinguished by a Z tattoo on each cheek as well as on her forehead. The triple scar was the mark of a Zektiv, an officer in the all-female Kogon tribe.

"No kill! No kill! No kill!" screamed Giv, staring up wildly at his grinning conquerors. "Have head!"

It was true. In a feat of extraordinary devotion, he had managed to keep hold of his grim trophy by its long white hair. It now lay beside him, staring up with sightless eyes and a fixed smirk on the rotting lips that glistened like slug trails.

"Wait!" ordered the Zektiv. She walked with lithe strides to where the head lay. "What's this?"

"Malik!" gasped Giv. "Master not dead! Giv have head!"

The woman frowned and swung the butt of her spear hard into Giv's exposed groin. Hearing their captive's howl, the women who held him hissed in satisfaction.

"Speak true!" demanded his inquisitor. "This is the head of a dead man – what man?"

"Malik," croaked Giv, looking up at his tormentor with eyes in which defiance danced with pleading.

"Malik? What Malik?"

"Great Malik! You not know great Malik?"

The heavy butt swung down, once again evoking a cacophony of howls and hisses. The Zektiv walked round to inspect the head more carefully. When she had done so, she lifted her spear for a third strike. "This thing a Malik?" she enquired.

Giv, though his hair was held firmly by two pairs of hands, attempted to nod. "Malik," he confirmed.

"Name of this Malik?"

"Timur!" croaked Giv, his voice harsh with sorrow, pain and fear. "Timur, Malik of Grozny!"

The hands that grasped him tightened and further shrill hissing escaped into the evening air. The Zektiv lowered her spear. "Malik Timur?" she smiled in disbelief. "Malik Timur is dead and a prisoner of the Kogon brings us his head? This is a good day, a very good day!"

She took a couple of steps back and issued crisp commands. "Tie the Zed dumbmans and bring them with me. Zilna?"

One of the women holding Jamshid raised her head. "Yes,

Jinsha?"

"Carry the Malik head. Come!"

The strange procession was soon on its way. Scouts, senses
alert to any danger, combed the woods on either side of the
path. Jinsha, lithe and athletic, walked at the head of the column,
followed by Zilna with the stinking head of Timur swinging
beside her. Behind them hobbled Giv and Jamshid. Their arms
were bound tight behind their backs and cords ran from their
ankles to Kogon warriors walking behind them. To make sure
they behaved, each man was flanked by two spear-carriers,
weapons permanently at the ready.

To survive in a Zed world dominated by ruthless males, the
Kogon had learned to take no chances. What they lacked in
physical strength, they made up for with caution and cunning.
Unlike male Zeds, they were not permanently on the move.
They liked to settle for several months in a small Long Dead
town, one that had been ransacked and abandoned. Careful
scavenging of buildings and gardens provided food and useful
materials. It was a dangerous and precarious existence, and the
Kogon's survival depended entirely on its supremely skilled
and intelligent leadership.

The Long Dead town of Filna perched on a hilltop surrounded
by dense woodland. The roads that had once linked it to
adjoining communities had long since grown over, leaving it a
small island of mossy brickwork amid a sea of trees. The ancient
piazza remained relatively clear of vegetation and the buildings
around it had the better part of their roofs intact. It was in one

of these, a cavernous structure adorned with slashed and faded paintings and broken statues, that the Kogon leadership had its headquarters.

It was almost dark by the time Jinsha's party arrived. They went straight to the piazza, forced Giv and Jamshid to their knees, and waited. All eyes focussed on a dark arched opening behind a stone balcony a few feet above the ground. After a while, a gibbous moon rose over the roofs opposite, casting a pale and ghostly light over the scene. The patrol waited. After a while, clouds again floated across the face of the moon and darkness palled the piazza. Still the patrol waited.

Finally, as moonlight once again flooded the piazza, a silhouette emerged out of the blackness behind the balcony. As it did so, the assembled Kogon hissed softly.

The form advanced into the light and became more distinct. Giv stared at the apparition in open-mouthed astonishment and wonder. Before his beloved Timur he used to tremble with fear and admiration. And now, only days after his hero's death, he was overcome with the same feeling of awful idolisation – for a woman, too! This was no breeding slave standing there in the moonlight, no despicable flabtoad. No, it was none other than a second Timur, a creature whose very presence exuded majesty, might and terror.

Flanked by her eunuch bodyguard of captured males, Xsani, Malika of the Kogon Zeds, stood on the balcony and surveyed the scene. "Yeth Jintha?" she said in a slow, menacing lisp. "Why are theth dumbmanth here?"

"They bring head of Malik Timur, O Malika," answered Jinsha.

Xsani glanced at the trophy at the Zektiv's feet. "Timur of the Grothny?"

"Yes, Malika."

"I will come down."

Xsani and her devoted bodyguard disappeared into the opening and reappeared shortly afterwards out of a door to the left of the balcony. Now she was on the same level as him, Giv saw that the ruler of the Kogon was not a tall woman. Her authority came from her confident bearing and quick bright eyes that darted hither and thither like restless sandflies. Beneath thick blonde hair, cut short, her oval, symmetrical face bore the triple Z tattoos of a Zektiv. Without them and in a different age and culture, she might have been considered beautiful.

The Malika stood before the two captives with her hands tucked into the broad sleeves of her loose, open-fronted gown of blue silk. She glanced from one to the other, summing them up before taking a step towards Jamshid. She looked down in utter contempt at his rough, ugly face and scarred body. Wadis of dried blood ran from the wounds inflicted at the time of his capture. But Timur had not made this man a Captain on the basis of looks. He had been chosen for his fearlessness, loyalty and basic common sense. In moments of crisis the two former qualities tended to outweigh the latter – and for Jamshid this was a moment of supreme crisis.

Kneeling in the piazza waiting for the Malika, the Captain's uneducated brain had attempted to take in what had happened. He had been captured by women – the shame of it! And this blonde dwarf was now standing over him and inspecting him as if he – Captain Jamshid of the famous Grozny – were nothing but a breeding slave! His ferocious courage, temporarily subdued by the goading in the woods, swelled back through him like a drug. He tugged at his bonds in angry frustration.

"Tho, dumbman," lisped Xsani, "you are a Grothny?"

"No, flabtoad!" roared Jamshid, rocking from side to side like a boat in choppy seas. "Captain Jamshid is Grozny. Groz-z-z-ny! Got it, you –"

Whatever Jamshid had in mind to say – if he had anything in mind – will never be known. In a single movement, Xsani took a leather whip from her sleeve and lashed it across his mouth. A further three blows fell, all merciless, all to the face. Jamshid, shocked into silence by the sudden fury of the assault, slumped forward onto the weed-strewn cobbles of the piazza. Xsani nodded with satisfaction, stopped to wipe the blood off the thongs of her whip on his hair, tucked the weapon back into her sleeve, and moved over to Giv.

"Dumbmanth are tho thtupid," she said, smiling down at him. "Don't you agree, Grothny?"

Giv was bewitched, spellbound. He nodded vigorously. "Yes – I mean yeth – O Malika!"

She smiled again. "You learn fatht for a dumbman. But do not copy my thpeech, fool. It ith thpecial, for Malika only, thee?"

Again Giv nodded furiously. "Yes, Giv see, O Malika."

She ignored him and, lifting Timur's head by the hair, held it before him. "You know thith, dumbman?"

Giv blinked. "That man not dum – er, Giv sorry! Giv very sorry!" he gabbled in panic. "That man – that, er, dumbman –

name Timur. My Malik."

"Wath your Malik, Giv. Wath your Malik. Tho, tell me how you came by thith ... object."

As best he could, Giv explained what he knew. He told how the Grozny had captured Roxanne, and Timur had learned something from her that interested him greatly, something about a 'Sotion' as Giv called it. When she escaped, Timur had spent many moons pursuing her. In the end, he had gone to the Constant settlement of Alba – Giv was unsure why but he thought it was to do with the 'Sotion'. From Alba, Timur had never returned.

"Giv leave Captain Jamshid – go look for Malik Timur," he concluded, "and find dead. In long hole. Giv cut off head and bring for Grozny. Grozny follow head of Malik Timur. Head powenful, O Malika! Timur head very powenful." As he ended, he looked pleadingly up into the face of the woman with whom he was already besotted.

Xsani had listened intently throughout the garbled tale. When it was over, she asked Giv a few more questions before congratulating Jinsha on bringing in these two dumbmans and their trophy. "I have learned much," she said. "Yeth, I think thith may lead thomewhere interethting. Very interethting."

"And now I kill the dumbmans, Malika?" enquired Jinsha.

Xsani took a hand from her sleeve and laid it rather gently on her Zektiv's shoulder. "Not Giv," she said. "He may live while we need him. But the other one..." She looked at Jamshid's lacerated face then at the head of Timur. "No, he may live too, Jintha. A Captain of the Grothny will be uthfull to me. Very uthfull.

"Come, Jintha. I need you inthide with me."

Taking the young Zektiv by the arm, she led her away. The bodyguard followed without a word.

3

Snakes

As soon as it was light, Cyrus entered the Ghasar and began sifting through the books brought up from the vault the previous day. He set aside four volumes: *Peter Pan*, the first book he had ever read; *The Odyssey*; his precious dictionary – and a new discovery. On its front, in large print and surrounded by photographs, it read, *An Illustrated Encyclopaedia for the Twenty-first Century*. He had recognised its value immediately. Using its clear articles and colourful images and diagrams, he started piecing together a new mosaic of the world.

It was a slow process. Much of the vocabulary required long and difficult searches through the dictionary. It was during one of these – a hunt for the meaning of 'syllabus' – that Yash and Sakamir came in, followed by Sammy and fourteen others.

"Hello Cyrus," said Yash, waving cheerily at the group behind him. "These are the Albans I've chosen to learn all about reading and writing."

Cyrus nodded. "Ah, so you meant it when you said you'll decide who I'll teach?" He was still annoyed that he'd been given so little say over who was to be in his class.

"Better that way," Yash replied. "I know them better than you, don't I?"

Seeing there was no point in arguing, Cyrus invited everyone to sit down and set about getting to know his students. The youngest were Jalus and Poso, Sakamir's four-year-old twins by a previous copemate. The rest of the group comprised Sammy, a boy and a girl of five, two nine-year-old boys, four twelve-year-olds, and four fifteen- and sixteen-year-olds. The latter were headed by Miouda, an attractive woman with thoughtful blue eyes, sandy hair and a broad mouth that spread easily into a smile. Although she had been in a relationship with a copemate for three years, Cyrus learned, she remained childless.

When they had introduced themselves, Yash explained his plan. "We – that's me and Sakamir and the others – we're the leaders, the special ones. We'll learn from you, then we'll pass on what we've learned to the rest of Alba. Simple, eh?"

Cyrus resisted the temptation to laugh at him. "Well, perhaps not simple, Yash," he said, "because learning to read and write is very difficult."

"Ah, but we're the clever ones, Cyrus. Like you, we'll learn fast."

"I'm sure you will. But how'll you teach the others? What's the plan?"

Yash waved his hand in a gesture of irritation. "Plan? Don't be boring, Cyrus. We'll deal with that when we get there. Now, let's start learning. The sooner you're not the only person who can read the secrets of the Long Dead, the better!"

Not exactly tactful, are you? thought Cyrus. Keeping such reflections to himself, he eagerly set about passing on the skills Roxanne had given him.

The first three days went fairly well. He enjoyed his new role as a teacher and his pupils were eager to learn. Sadly, their enthusiasm wasn't always matched by their ability. Poso, despite help from the kindly Miouda, had difficulty concentrating. One of the nine-year-olds left after the first day, saying he'd rather learn how to be a warrior so he could kill Zeds.

The biggest problem was Yash. His interest in weapons had been replaced by a new obsession. They had not been at work long, learning the huge letters Cyrus wrote on the back wall with a piece of chalky stone, when he called out, "When can we get on to that Salmation thing, Cyrus? That's what really matters, not all this letters stuff."

Cyrus breathed deeply. "We can't do anything until we can read, Yash," he said calmly. "Wherever this Salvation Project is – whatever it is – it won't be any use until we're literate."

"Hang on," frowned Yash. "You mean you don't know where it is?"

"I imagine it's written in one of these books," said Cyrus, indicating the piles heaped up on the floor. "It may take a long time to find. That's why you all need to learn to read – to help me."

The conversation was cut short by Sakamir. Frowning, she leaned across to her copemate and whispered something in his ear. Yash shrugged and fixed his eyes on the large letter d on the wall behind Cyrus. Similar interruptions came at regular intervals. Not surprisingly, when Cyrus began stringing letters together into words, the Emir was one of the slowest to grasp what they said.

In contrast to their leader, three students stood out. By the end of the fourth day, Sakamir, Sammy and Miouda were able to read their names and a dozen other simple words. A fierce competition developed between them. When either of the younger two grasped a word before Sakamir, she threw them a glance of conspicuous loathing. They both noticed it. To Cyrus' delight, they goaded her further by laughing and redoubling their efforts to outdo her. The room crackled with unspoken rivalry.

The tension within was less than that outside, however. It came to a head on the morning of the fifth day, when Bahm strode into the Ghasar and demanded to speak to the Emir.

Yash stood and turned to face him. "Yes, Bahm? What do you want?"

"You!" bellowed the furious Konnel. He looked around the hall. "Excuse me," he went on, struggling to control himself, "but we chose Yash to be our leader. Now we never sees him!

"Emir, there's decisions to be made while you're sitting here staring at that there scribble on the wall. A while back one of the Patrol Gate guards noticed movement in the woods. About a thousand paces distant, it were. It may have been nothing, of course, or perhaps only an animal. But it could've been a Zed. And if there's one, there's hundreds of 'em. That's danger, that is."

He paused to let his words take effect. "The point is, we don't know. And we can't know until we sends out patrols. And who gives the command for that, Yash? It's you, isn't it? We needs our Emir outside, not in here with all this daft talk of living for ever."

The meaning of this last remark became clear to Cyrus later. Apparently Yash had boasted that he was going to find the Salvation Project and be the first Constant to live to one hundred.

Yash might not have shone in the classroom, but his skills as a leader of warriors were undeniable. He looked Bahm straight in the eye and said carefully, "I hear what you say, Konnel, and I will consider it. But take care! He who challenges an Emir challenges the whole of Alba. I believe you spoke in good faith, so this will go no further. But it'll stop, got it?"

"Yes, Emir."

"Duty, Bahm! Duty! Now leave and I'll join you in a moment to see about this patrol."

Bahm nodded and left the hall. Yash, after a quick word with Sakamir, followed. Cyrus sensed there was no point in going on and dismissed the rest of the class.

As she was leaving, Miouda asked Cyrus whether she could borrow one of the simpler books to help her with her reading.

"But you've only just learned the letters," he said. "Are you ready for a whole book?"

"I can try to read one. Like you're doing."

"But I've got my dictionary." He thought for a second. "And do you think we'd better ask Yash?"

"Ask him what?"

"About taking books out of the Ghasar."

She looked directly into his eyes. "What's it got to do with him?"

He smiled and looked at her carefully, almost for the first time. Her neat figure and sandy-coloured hair were not so unusual, he thought. It was the way kindness and seriousness combined with an unexpected strength in her clear blue eyes that distinguished her from the other Alban women he had met. She alone appeared to grasp the significance of what he was trying to do.

He forced his mind back to the matter in hand. "Well, Yash's the Emir, Miouda. Best to keep him on our side."

"Maybe. But he won't know, will he?"

Cyrus grinned and slipped the copy of *Peter Pan* into her hands. "No. He won't. And maybe you could come and read in here. You could use the dictionary to look up words you don't understand."

"Thank you, Cyrus. I'd really like that." Sensing that the conversation had gone far enough, she thanked him and hurried towards the door. I hope her copemate is worthy of her, thought Cyrus as he watched her leave. She's special and deserves to be appreciated.

Over the next few days, neither Miouda nor any others in the class progressed as rapidly as he had hoped. It was not through lack of effort or enthusiasm but because of a decision made by Yash after Bahm's intervention. From that day onwards, he announced, reading classes would take place only between sunhigh and early evening. That way, he said, he had plenty of time left for his duties as Emir.

Bahm and some of the other Konnels welcomed the decision. Yash himself seemed relieved – although he never admitted it, he wasn't really cut out for what he called 'scribble'. Sakamir was, though. And every day, Cyrus noticed, her obsession with the Soterion grew. It was like a new partner to her, one she wanted all for herself.

The Bahm incident reminded Cyrus again of the need for tact. If he was to get anywhere, he had to show that the Soterion meant hope and unity, not anger and division. He also needed physical activity. So, in an attempt to patch up his relationship with Yash, he volunteered to go out on patrol.

"Not yet, Cyrus," was the enigmatic reply. "Alba needs you alive, my friend. It'd be daft of me to let you go wandering off outside the walls when we haven't even found this Salmation Project."

Once more, Cyrus decided not to argue. Instead, he worked off his frustration by working furiously on the terraces. He returned to the Ghasar as the light was starting to fade. Having settled himself comfortably, he took up the encyclopaedia and began flicking through the pages to find a word that had been troubling him for some time. No sooner had he found it than he was interrupted by Sammy bursting into the hall as if he had a whole tribe of Zeds on his heels.

"Thought I'd find you 'ere, Mister Cyrus," he panted, slamming the door and leaning up against it. "Got somethink what you ought to know."

He had just returned from his first training patrol, he

explained. All the others were proper archers and it was really exciting. They didn't see any Zeds, but he did find something else. They'd gone along the ravine where Timur's body had been thrown. They had seen the corpse but hadn't gone near for fear of disease. Rotting flesh was known to attract flies and other insects whose bite was extremely poisonous.

"Well, the others mightn't have been keen to take a look, but I was. I've only got one eye what works, but it's pretty good and I could see Timur didn't look quite right. Peculiar, I thought. I'll just go and take a peep.

"I hadn't got very far when the bloke in charge yells at me to come back. I did, pretty sharpish. But I'd already took a good look at the body. It was chewed up alright, Mister Cyrus. That was animals. But what else I saw weren't done by no animals. Guess what it was?"

Cyrus looked puzzled. "I don't know, Sammy. Had someone tried to preserve it, like Roxanne mentioned…"

"No, nothing like that. Opposite. His head was missing. Cut right off!"

Cyrus frowned. "Are you sure, Sammy?"

"Sure as I ain't going back to that Gova lot, Mister Cyrus. It was neat, too. Like it'd been done with a knife or something."

Strange, thought Cyrus. Who'd want a mouldy head? It didn't tie in with anything he'd seen or heard. In the end, after he'd talked the matter over with Sammy a bit more, he decided that either his friend had been mistaken or some animal had bitten the head off neatly and dragged it away to eat elsewhere.

Only later, after Sammy had gone, did he discover the true significance of the news.

He had returned to the encyclopaedia and, reading by the blood-red glow of the sunset, was trying to make sense of the entry on 'religion'. The dense language of 'belief systems' and 'spirituality' made little sense to him and he skimmed further down the page. There, under the heading 'Totem', a grisly photograph caught his eye. His face tensed. Beneath the image was a long caption. Slowly, frequently resorting to the dictionary, he read to the end.

When Cyrus had finished, he set the book aside and gazed up at the wooden roof. He had noticed something up there during the trial of Padmar, a strange shape carved on the end of one of the beams. He looked more carefully now. It was a human head. He glanced back at the picture of the totem, then up at the carving once more. If a Constant had made a totem, why couldn't a Zed? He shook his head. It was ridiculous. Zeds were far too stupid to think of anything like that. Yet Timur hadn't been stupid. Far from it...

He returned to the encyclopaedia and re-read the caption. "A carving or, occasionally, an object like a human head. A totem is often worshipped and may inspire to action those who hold it...". Though unsure of the meaning of 'worshipped', Cyrus knew very well what 'inspire to action' meant. He cursed under his breath. How feeble he'd been! Far too polite by not insisting that they burn the monster's body along with the others. He had trouble enough within Alba. The last thing he wanted was an outside threat as well.

The thickening darkness outside mirrored the fearful significance of Sammy's discovery. If the head had been cut off by someone who understood how to use it, as was very likely, it meant serious trouble. The Grozny knew the Albans had killed Timur, and they would want revenge. Revenge of the Zeds.

Since moving into the large empty building beside the piazza in Filna, Malika Xsani had often pondered what purpose it had served in Long Dead times. It might have been used for storage, a sort of barn. She had come across these in her youth when the Kogon, under her predecessor's leadership, had sacked a small Constant settlement after cleverly breaching its defences. She liked barns, as did all Zeds, because they provided loot. But had her Filna headquarters ever been a barn? Though it was as big as one, it had strange decorations. The Long Dead were not fools, so why had they filled a barn with pictures, statues and symbols?

There was also writing carved on stone slabs. As Xsani was illiterate and had never yet captured a Constant able to read and write, she had no idea how to interpret these mysterious symbols. There were larger symbols, too. Many of them showed what looked like a Constant-style sword whose blade was not sharpened to a point.

At some time in the past, a fire had raged inside the barn. It had burned a jagged hole in the roof, destroyed most of the pictures and left broad black smears both inside and out. Only a large image painted on the wall furthest from the flames remained reasonably intact. Even this had been partially obliterated where rain had streamed in through a missing window. Despite the damage, Xsani was fascinated by it.

On the left lay a rather thin, pale and feeble-looking dumbman. He was wearing what looked like a circular yellow hat and appeared to be dead. He was accompanied by a small group of women, all of whom looked miserable. In contrast, a crowd of women and bearded dumbmen to the right of the rain damage looked ecstatically happy. Xsani couldn't decide whether they were happy because the pale dumbman had died or whether they were pleased to see him even though he was dead. By the way the figures were arranged, it looked like the latter.

It was all most peculiar! The Malika understood all about crowds lost in awe and delight at the presence of a living person – her own Kogon were like that with her – but to be transported by a corpse… It just didn't make sense. At least, it had not made sense until her conversation with Giv.

What had the dumbman said? "Timur head very powerful." Lying awake with one arm round the sleeping Jinsha, Xsani conjured up in her mind's eye the image from the barn wall. She imagined Timur's head replacing that of the pale dumbman with the round hat. Over on the right, the throng was now transfixed by the dead Malik.

Almost immediately, another of Giv's phrases returned to her: "Grozny follow head of Malik Timur." Her mind whirled. The Grozny follow the head, she has the head in her possession, so if she handles this right the Grozny will follow her... What did the ugly one say he was? A Captain, the Grozny equivalent

61

of a Zektiv. Useful. She could use this pair to unite the fighting power of the Grozny with that of the Kogon. It was risky, but worth a try.

Whatever this 'Sotion' thing was, it must be extraordinary for Timur to have entered a Constant settlement alone in search of it. The Kogon couldn't hope to breach the famous Alban defences on their own, but with the Grozny... And once she had an alliance with them, she could use the power of Timur's head to draw other Zed tribes into her coalition...

But she was getting ahead of herself. First the head, then the Grozny. Knowing exactly what she had to do, Xsani smiled to herself, withdrew her arm from Jinsha's smooth shoulder, lay flat on her back with her hands behind her head, closed her eyes, and slept like a Long Dead queen.

Cyrus had realised the potential power of Timur's head at almost the same time as Malika Xsani. It was one of those strange coincidences that leads people to believe that supernatural forces control their lives. While Xsani saw the grisly totem as a key to greater power, Cyrus feared it would bring only misery. He knew nothing of the Kogon or their charismatic leader, but he did know about the Grozny. From his experience in Della Tallis and on the mission, as well as from what Roxanne had told him, he knew them to be an erratic but dangerous enemy.

Whatever he thought of the man, it was his duty to tell Yash of Sammy's discovery and what it might mean. He hurried over to the Emiron, the building specially reserved for the Emir and their copemate. Yash was eating alone, Sakamir having gone to visit her twins, Jalus and Poso. All Alban children over the age of two, even those of the Emir, lived in a communal hostel.

Cyrus insisted that Yash went on eating while he explained what he had learned. "That's why I advised you to burn Timur's body," he concluded. "It would have stopped the Grozny using it."

Yash ran a hand through his matted red hair, a sure sign he was anxious or confused. "Use it?" he asked. "They'd be more likely to eat it."

Cyrus shook his head in frustration. "Don't you see, Yash? Someone's cut off Timur's head and carried it off. It must be the Grozny." Yash looked blank. "They cut – off – his – head," Cyrus repeated, heavily stressing the last word. "The head of their dead Malik. Even the Grozny don't eat heads. They obviously want it for something, and I've read in the encyclopaedia –"

Yash stood up. "You know what, Cyrus," he interrupted, wiping his fingers on the front of his tunic, "I sometimes think Bahm has a point. All that reading's not good for you. It gets you thinking too much, and that's not healthy."

Cyrus stared at him in disbelief. "I don't believe I'm hearing this, Yash. After all I've been through, all we've been through … and now you seem to be saying it was not worth it? Come on!"

Again the Emir passed a hand through his hair. "Don't get me wrong, Cyrus. Of course it was worth it. I'm completely on your side. But we must keep our eyes on the target, mustn't we?"

"The target?"

"Yes, the Salvation Project. The thing that'll let us live – as you yourself said – as long as the Long Dead."

Cyrus clenched his fists. "Will you stop going on about the Salvation Project, Yash? I've told you before, we don't even know it exists. It may well be just a legend."

Even as he was speaking, Cyrus knew anger would get him nowhere. However infuriating the Emir might be, he couldn't afford to fall out with him.

"Sorry, Yash," he said with a shake of the head. "Got a bit too worked up, didn't I? Anyway, I'll keep searching for the Project. But I'm sure you know that even if it does exist and we find it, we'll still have to learn everything the Long Dead knew before it'll be of any use. That'll take a long time, probably more time than you and I have."

"What'll take a long time, Cyrus?" It was Sakamir, gliding noiselessly over the dusty threshold into the room. "I hope you and the Emir are not arguing?"

"Arguing?" queried Yash, clearly embarrassed by the interruption. "We were just discussing, that's all."

Sakamir turned to Cyrus. "I suppose he was on about the Salvation Project again?" Her teeth flashed in a smile, while her eyes, flinty-grey like an animal's, remained cold. With her long brown hair fastened tightly behind her head, she gave an even stronger impression than usual of a sharp-toothed rodent. He did not find her attractive.

"He's obsessed with it, isn't he?"

Yash rose to the bait. "I wish you wouldn't interfere, Sakamir," he snapped. "Cyrus is here to tell me about something Sammy has discovered."

Sakamir raised a thin eyebrow. "Sammy? What's he found, Cyrus?"

Cyrus looked across at Yash and, receiving a reluctant nod of consent, explained how his young friend had found Timur's decapitated corpse. It might mean nothing, of course. On the other hand, an intelligent Grozny leader could use the head. Seeking revenge for the death of their leader, they could make it a totem. It would inspire them.

"If I were Emir," Cyrus concluded, "I'd send out a patrol to seize that disgusting head and destroy it."

As he was speaking, he experienced a surge of excitement at the prospect of action. "In fact, Yash," he said eagerly, "I'd like to lead this patrol. I've as much experience as anyone and no one knows the Grozny better than me."

Sakamir, who had listened carefully to his every word, said nothing. Her thin face remained inscrutable. Yash was more forthcoming. "Come off it, Cyrus! That's not on. Look, let me give you a bit of friendly advice. We all know you're still the only one who can read properly. Yes, you've come on this great mission and opened the Soterion and all that. But don't let it go to your head. Lots of us can do important things. And I'm the Emir – I was the people's choice, don't forget, not you."

Feeling he had gone a bit too far, he added with a chuckle, "Anyway, they couldn't have chosen you, could they? You're not an Alban."

Once more Cyrus fought to control himself in the face of Yash's obstinate stupidity. "You're right there," he said coolly. "I'm not an Alban."

"So let's settle this business once and for all. I'd hate anything to come between us – you know that." Again, the fingers through the hair. "Right. You have an interesting theory – but no, I'm not sending archers into the unknown on some wild harechase to find the mouldy head of a dead Zed! And even if I did allow a patrol, there is no way I'd let you go on it. We've been over that before."

Cyrus shook his head. "Alright, Yash. As you say, you're the Emir and it's your call. But I'd like to put on record, with Sakamir here as my witness, that I think you're making a mistake. Destroying the head can do no harm. Not doing so may have serious consequences. That's all. Let's hope Sammy was wrong and the wretched thing really was carried off by animals."

It was the best Cyrus could do. He could only warn – and hope that one day Yash would listen. Besides, as he reminded himself almost daily, he had no official authority in Alba. Like everyone else, he had to obey the elected Emir. Experience in combat had taught him that tactical withdrawal meant he would live to fight another day.

He had other issues to consider, too. Miouda and Sammy had warned him of rumours spreading around the settlement. Cyrus controlled Yash, the whispers went, just as Timur had controlled Padmar. The talk had started with Bahm and his friends. Albans like him, the traditional backbone of the community, were worried by the way their lives were being wrenched out of their familiar channels. Insecurity bred fear, and fear made people irrational and violent. These were tricky times. Hard though he found it, Cyrus concluded, he must continue to curb his warrior's instinct for swift decisions and actions. Those talents would be needed again – but for the time being he must play the politician.

On his way back to the Ghasar, he mused afresh on the subject of the missing head. Where on earth was it? Who'd taken it and why? He'd really like to lead a patrol to find the answers. Books and reading were marvellous – but he'd been brought up on physical activity, and he missed it. Contemplating the two halves of his life, he smiled to himself. Did books reflect the real world, he wondered, like an image in a mirror? Or was the world around him a reflection of the ideas in books? It was an interesting question, but not one he'd expect the Emir to answer for him.

The following afternoon's lessons went well. Yash and Sakamir, as if to show they had no hard feelings against Cyrus, were particularly attentive. Sakamir was unusually friendly towards Sammy and Miouda, too. The three co-operated to scratch out their first sentence – We live in Alba – on a broad flat stone that Cyrus had set up in a corner of the Ghasar.

As the sun neared the ridge above the terraces, Cyrus ended the class and settled down to have another go at *The Odyssey*. It was tough work. 'Nymph', 'marry', 'goddess' – the list of new words went on and on. And even when he'd looked them up he wasn't much wiser. Odysseus inhabited an alien world, not at all how Cyrus imagined the Long Dead to have lived. Tormented by strange gods and goddesses – whatever they were – the characters of *The Odyssey* didn't appear to control their lives.

He had just reached a passage about the 'goddess of the flashing eyes', a phrase he rather liked, when he heard the door of the Ghasar creak open. Hoping it was Miouda wanting to do some extra reading, he didn't look up. Light footsteps approached across the dusty floor – it was a woman. Good. He certainly didn't want another row with Yash.

Cyrus kept his eyes on his book as the figure hesitated, then moved round behind him. His heart sank. Miouda wouldn't do that. A thin female form slid down beside him and fingers ran lightly, almost accidentally, across the back of his neck. He had felt that touch before.

"Hello Sakamir," he said, trying to sound nonchalant. "Come to join me in my studying?"

"Possibly, Cyrus." The voice was thicker than usual, slower. Though she was trying hard, Cyrus thought, it only made her less attractive.

"Can we talk?" The stroking on his neck was clearly not accidental. He had to respond.

"I've just been reading about someone like you, Sakamir," he said, setting aside his book. "She was called Calypso."

"Ca-lyp-so," she repeated slowly, her hand still round Cyrus' neck. "I like the name. What was she?"

"She was a nymph – I think that's a sort of goddess." Sakamir looked at him quizzically. "I'll explain all that later," he went on. "But she was very beautiful."

"Is that why you think I'm like her?"

"Partly," Cyrus lied, starting to move away. Her hand fell from his neck and rested on his arm, restraining him. "Look,

68

Sakamir, you're Yash's copemate and I wouldn't want him getting the wrong –"

"Huh! Yash doesn't get anything unless it's pushed in front of his face."

Cyrus ignored the remark. "Why've you come to see me, Sakamir? What d'you want?"

She gave him one of her dead-eyed smiles and let go of his arm. "Don't worry, Cyrus. It's not you I'm after – though that would be nice, wouldn't it?"

He chose not to reply.

"It's about what you said yesterday, about Timur's head and the need to get it back. Yash didn't see what you meant, of course, but I found it fascinating."

Cyrus resisted the temptation to ask her straight out where this was leading. "And?"

She paused theatrically before saying, in a voice heavy with flattery, "You were right, Cyrus. We should try to get it back."

The satisfaction of finding himself with such a powerful ally was overshadowed by doubt. He stared at her, trying to read what was going on behind those inscrutable rodent eyes. "You agree with me?"

"Of course. And I've got a suggestion I think you'll like. Because you're too valuable to go on this patrol yourself" – another flattering, expressionless smile – "I'll lead it myself."

He looked away for a moment to hide his surprise. Why was she doing this?

"Despite what Yash said?" he asked, turning back towards her and searching her face in vain for a clue as to her motive.

"Yash won't know, Cyrus. It'll be our little secret – just you and me and the three I take with me. I think three's enough, don't you? We'll choose them carefully. I'll tell Yash it's just a regular scouting patrol, nothing special."

Cyrus' mind raced. She really had thought it through, hadn't she? He'd heard she was skilled in fieldcraft, so the plan might work. But what was she up to? Had she really changed her mind and seen the need to stop the Grozny getting hold of Timur's head? Or was she – with or without Yash – working on some scheme of her own to harvest the power of the Soterion?

Despite doubts nagging him like a splinter, he saw there was no point in challenging her now. He'd take her at her word, see what happened, and if he found hard evidence of something odd going on, he'd deal with it there and then.

"Alright," he said, "if you don't mind keeping it from your copemate and it's really what you want to do, then count me in. I'll do whatever I can to help. As long as," he added quickly, "you let me choose one of the patrol members."

He watched her closely as she met his eye and nodded. "Of course, Cyrus. As I said, we're in this together, aren't we?"

Yes we are, he thought. But only in so far as it suits each of us. Taking care not to reveal too much, he explained more precisely than before his worries about Timur's missing head, adding what he had learned about totems and the habits and customs of the Grozny. She listened intently, giving every impression of sincerity.

"Thank you, Cyrus," she said when he had finished. "It's a pleasure to work with someone so, well, so intelligent."

Poor Yash! he thought. He doesn't stand a chance. But Sakamir had been his choice, just as wanting to be Emir had been. There was no point in feeling sorry for someone strung up by their own ambition.

"So," she went on, "what about the personnel? I thought you might want me to take Miouda. She's bright enough."

There she goes again! Testing, teasing. He knew she didn't like Miouda. The two were rivals in learning and, he suspected, Sakamir was irritated by his obvious personal regard for the younger and more attractive woman. No, he certainly didn't want the pair of them out in the wilderness together.

"Miouda?" he echoed. "You can do better than that, Sakamir! Miouda's a bit feeble, physically, I mean. Not tough enough for a difficult patrol."

She gave him a curious glance. "Maybe. In which case, I'll take that young friend of yours."

"Sammy?"

Was there no end to her guile? Not so long ago she'd said Sammy was unfit to be an archer because of his eyesight. Now she wanted him on a high-risk patrol with her. It was a tricky one. He didn't like the thought of putting his friend in unnecessary danger, but Sammy was pretty resourceful and would be ideal to find out what the patrol was really all about.

"Yes, Sammy," she repeated.

He thought for a moment longer before agreeing. "Alright. He's my choice, too."

The other two members of the patrol were quickly agreed. One was Jannat, the tall archer who had befriended Taja. The second was Potr, a man Cyrus hadn't met. He was, Sakamir assured him, a reliable and brave warrior.

The rest of the plan fell into place almost too easily. Yash raised no objection when Sakamir proposed leading a small, six-day patrol to investigate suspicious movements reported close to where Cyrus' mission had first entered Alban territory. Sakamir recruited Potr without difficulty. Neither Sammy nor Jannat liked the idea of going beyond the walls with their Emir's scornful copemate, but they accepted after Cyrus had spoken with them privately – and assured Sammy that he would look after Corby. It might be an interesting mission, he suggested.

"Interesting, Cyrus?" questioned Sammy, glancing at Jannat.

"I think it might have time to look for, er, something that's missing, Sammy."

A broad grin spread across the young man's face. "Got it! So it's a bit of a secret?"

"Yes. You may tell Jannat what Sakamir may be looking for, but please no one else."

"Sealed like the Soterion, Cyrus. 'Silent Sam' – that's what my mates called me back home."

Cyrus smiled. "And Sammy – this applies to you as well, Jannat – please take care." He paused. "I'm not sure how to say this, and I may be wrong of course, but Zeds might not be the only danger out there."

Jannat frowned. "You mean –"

"Yes," interrupted Cyrus. "No names, but you know who I mean. She's pretty poisonous."

"Don't you worry," said Sammy. "Thing about poisonous snakes is to watch where you're walking."

If only it were so easy, thought Cyrus. Some snakes you can't see until it's too late.

4

The Head

For six days after the capture of Jamshid and Giv, Malika Xsani's eunuchs stood before her door, as still and smooth as pieces on a Long Dead chess board. Only the faithful Jinsha was permitted to pass. Each morning, Tarangala and Yalisha, the other senior Zektivs, waited outside for the day's orders. Of the Malika herself there was not a whisper, not a glimpse, not a shadow. The sole indication of her presence was a cloud of woodsmoke billowing from broken windows beside the balcony overlooking the piazza.

Unlike the Grozny, the Kogon were tightly disciplined. When not on the move, they lived to a fixed and severe routine. This was the key to their survival – and to their Malika's power. From the age of five, when they were branded with their Z tattoo, the tribe's two hundred females were taught to fight. Not for them the wild Grozny charge. Under Xsani's leadership they went into combat only when necessary and always from an ambush. The tactics never changed: identify a force smaller than their own, surround it and goad its members to death or submission. As with all Zed tribes, victory was celebrated with a feast. For the Kogon's male opponents the ceremony involved their prisoners' most intimate and delicate organs.

Of all this, the two Grozny prisoners knew nothing. During Xsani's retreat, they were kept literally in the dark, chained to the concrete floor of a shed in which the Long Dead had kept pigs. Their only glimpse of daylight came when a shuttered window was opened wide enough for food – largely unwashed root vegetables – to be thrown in.

Though they saw nothing, Jamshid and Giv heard much. From a pen on the other side of the piazza came the howls and curses of the Kogon's six male breeding slaves, all Zed prisoners. On the second day, they recognised the sounds of a woman giving birth in a room on their left. And each morning, shortly after the first light of dawn had filtered under the door of their cell, they were aware of a mysterious ritual in the piazza outside.

"What that?" muttered Jamshid the first time he heard the shuffling and flapping of bare feet on the cobblestones. "Flabtoads dancing?"

Giv frowned. "What dancing, Jamshid?"

"Giv not know? Giv ratbrain!" To confirm his superiority, the Captain aimed a kick in Giv's direction. The manacles round his ankle brought him up short and he growled in pain and frustration.

Giv said nothing. For a while they sat in silence. Outside, the slapping and panting continued, punctuated by the occasional cry of pain.

Jamshid finally said, "Ratbrain not asking?"

"Who ratbrain?"

"Giv ratbrain."

Again Giv did not reply. Eventually, Jamshid could contain himself no longer. "Flabtoads dancing. Boom-boom leaping like spitfest."

"Ah!" The definition, though hardly scholarly, was clear enough. To dance was to throw oneself about in a wild, rhythmic manner as the Grozny did during a feast of the spit that celebrated victory. Giv enjoyed spitfests.

Jamshid was wrong about the noise. It was not dancing but training. To keep up her tribe's fighting power, the Malika insisted every morning be devoted to battle skills. Only the tattoo-less under-fives, the heavily pregnant, those on lookout duty and those in their Death Month were exempt. Wearing short leather skirts, the scarred, hard-faced warriors skipped, lunged and hissed until they could take no more. Every movement was precise and concerted. The heavy-footed and clumsy were identified shortly after their zed-branding and either disposed of or set aside for breeding. When success depended on perfect teamwork, there was no room for imperfection.

After their tenth winter, pairs of warriors might become 'Eyes'. These were lookouts positioned deep in the woods. They were responsible for telling the Malika immediately when any hostile force approached. She then decided whether to fight or flee. If fight, the intruders were ambushed and eliminated.

Flight meant slipping silently off into the forest like wraiths, leaving not a wrack behind. This explained why the Kogon were largely unknown to both Constant and Zed. No one ever saw them; or, if they did, they either died or disappeared. Some Constant communities told stories of mysterious 'Fairy-Zeds' living in the woods.

Among male Zeds, only the Malik and his successor were educated. The Kogon were different. Captured Constants taught all Zektivs to speak clearly, count and, to a certain extent, think logically. The Malika was careful to limit this learning so it didn't threaten her dominance. The exception was Jinsha. The youngest and smartest of the Zektivs, she was Xsani's kumfort and her heir.

On the fourth day of her seclusion, Xsani summoned Jinsha and gave her a curious task. "You'll find them growing bethide the wall, Jintha," she said. "Eathy to thee. Bring me a bathketfull."

The bright-eyed young woman followed the command without difficulty and by mid-morning had handed a brimming basket to her mistress. "Perfect," she smiled, laying a cool palm against the smooth face of her kumfort. "Tho thweetly reliable."

Jamshid and Giv's isolation ended on the fifth evening of their captivity. At sundown, the door of their cell opened to admit Tarangala and Yalisha carrying an iron grate looted from a Long Dead fireplace. Carefully they placed it in the centre of the room, just out of range of Jamshid's thrashing feet. Giv stared in bemused silence. When the grate was in place, the two women left.

Jamshid stared at the purple-brown scabs covering his ambush wounds and sulked. "Flabtoad breeding slaves laugh at me!" he grumbled.

Giv ignored him. "What that?" he asked, nodding towards the grate.

"Jamshid not know; Jamshid not care!"

"Oh? Who ratbrain now?"

Before the Captain could rise to the bait, Tarangala returned with an armful of dry sticks. She arranged them carefully beneath the grate. When she had finished, she stood looking down at Jamshid with incomprehension and scorn. He returned her gaze with salacious loathing. Yalisha then brought in the leaves Jinsha had gathered two days earlier and laid them on the grate. They were drier, orangey-brown and curling at the edges.

When all was prepared, Jinsha herself came in carrying a flaming brand. The two Zektivs stood beside her, one on either side.

"Timur lives!" said Tarangala quietly.

"Timur comes!" said Yalisha, a little louder.

"Timur speaks!" chanted Jinsha.

As she did so, the youngest Zektiv knelt and lit the sticks under the grate. The three women left, locking the door but opening the shutter just a fraction. Soon the small room was filled with thick, acrid smoke. It hovered and curled round the heads of the two bewildered Zeds before drifting lazily out of the opening into the evening air.

"Flabtoads cook us," coughed Jamshid.

Giv appeared not to hear. "They say Timur live," he muttered, staring wide-eyed into the dancing flames. "Timur live!"

Jamshid blinked. By now the swirling smoke was distorting his vision. His fellow prisoner was no longer a battered body pierced by scabbed wounds but a warrior-bird, swelling and rising magnificently into the air. Jamshid himself rose, shaking off his chains and flying around the room like an enormous black bat.

"Timur come," he whispered. "Timur set Jamshid free!"

"Timur set Giv free!" echoed his companion, his face split by an idiotic grin.

Lost in wonder, Jamshid lay on his back repeating, "Timur come, Timur come, Timur come!" over and over again. Above him, the ceiling cracked open to reveal the vast and purple canopy of the sky.

For a while, the two men lay there wreathed in vapour, muttering incoherently. Neither was aware of the door opening. But gradually, through the smoke, they sensed a third presence in the room. Some distance from the fire, shrouded in dense fumes, a hooded figure stood motionless. With arms outstretched, as if offering a gift, it held forth a wrinkled orb draped about with a lank blackness. Jamshid rubbed his bloodshot eyes and stared. Slowly, very slowly, the figure glided silently nearer the fire. As the flickering light played on the orb, the Captain noticed three dark holes, deep and unfathomable, in its surface.

Giv, unsure whether he was awake or asleep, stared open-mouthed at the apparition. The black openings grew larger, drawing him in. The smoke was thicker, more opaque. His mind reeled. He shivered. What was that? A voice. The thing was speaking to him!

"Giv! Giv! Giv!"

From far off, he heard himself answer, "Here. Giv here!"

"Do you not know me, Giv? I am come back! Look on me! Look!"

Giv peered into the blanket of the dark. The shape was familiar, but the colour... White had become black, smooth had become wrinkled. He looked closer. Yes, changed but the same!

"Ma-li-k!" he cried in a strangled combination of terror and ecstasy. "Malik Timur come back!"

Jamshid, slower of mind than the younger Grozny, took a little longer to grasp what was happening. When he did, he too was reduced to idiotic quivering and dribbling.

"Ti-mur, Ti-mur! Ti-mur!" the two men chorused until the phantom interrupted them.

"You see, Giv and Captain Jamshid? I am Malik Timur and I am returned in my head from the dead. Keep my head. Guard my head. Follow my head. Listen to it!

"My power made you save me. My power brought you to these flabtoads. They are good flabtoads with whom I am well pleased. Join with them, fight with them, kill with them! I am in their Malika – follow her! Follow her and you follow me!

"I am Timur the Terrible! I live for ever! Hear me! Hear me! Hear me!"

The phrase grew quieter and quieter as the spectre retreated into the obscurity and vanished.

Even for someone as clever as Malika Xsani, it was a stroke of brilliance. Jamshid and Giv, befuddled by the smoke from the burning leaves, were totally taken in. Though never permitted to go around unescorted and still locked in their sty at night, they were for the time being among Xsani's most devout supporters.

Giv, smitten by Xsani the first time he saw her, regarded her with an almost religious devotion. She was, after all, the living embodiment of Timur – the head had told him so. He stood by her door at dawn every morning, whatever the weather, waiting for her to appear. During the day, he was delighted to fetch, carry, dig and delve at her command. To eliminate any risk he might pose, Jinsha suggested he be castrated and added to the ranks of the bodyguard. The Malika agreed to keep that as an option. For the time being, though, she wanted him intact as a sort of experiment: could a Zed dumbman ever be trusted?

Jamshid, older and less imaginative, had simply taken his blind, lumbering obedience to Timur and extended it to the leader of the Kogon. As he had been prepared to die for the Malik, so now he was prepared to die for the Malika. After the vision in the sty, he believed them to be one and the same. Though potentially more dangerous, he was left alone for the time being. Xsani had work for him.

Just four of the Kogon – Jinsha, Tarangala, Yalisha and the Malika herself – understood the deception carried out that night. Only Xsani and her kumfort knew its full secrets. The leader had learned of the power of the leaves from a Constant prisoner. The idea of preserving Timur's head by smoking it was Jinsha's. To ensure it never rotted, she had hooked out the brains through the nose, and for several weeks after the miracle of the sty she hung it in wood smoke to complete its preservation.

Giv's remark about Timur's head being 'very powerful' had set Xsani thinking. Inspiration had come from studying the image of the pale dumbman in the peculiar yellow hat. Gradually, the pieces had come together to form a plan of infinite subtlety. With the cult of Timur established, she would cast its spell over her own people and over the Grozny. After that, she would spread the net wider and wider until it covered a mighty coalition of Zeds. In the face of such power, Alba would fall and she would seize the 'Sotion'. Where even the mighty Timur had failed, Malika Xsani would triumph. On that glorious day, all Zeds and all Constants would be under her supreme command.

The Kogon were easily brought on board. On a moonlit evening a week after the first presentation of the head, the tribe assembled in the piazza. Only the Eyes and three women nearing the end of their Death Month were missing. The unbranded were positioned at the front. The Zektivs, strategically placed round the edge in case of trouble, maintained strict discipline with leather whips. To prepare them for their part in the show, Giv and Jamshid were given a second infusion of leaf smoke.

When it was quite dark, the eight bare-chested eunuchs of Xsani's bodyguard emerged onto the balcony carrying flaming torches. A short while afterwards, to the sound of a long-drawn-out hiss from her people, the Malika joined them. She wore the same gown of blue silk she had been wearing on the day of the ambush. By torchlight it flashed and shone like polished stone.

She raised her arms and the hissing subsided. "Thith ith a thpecial time," she began, speaking slowly and deliberately.

"The Thedth are rithing up – and we thall lead them!" Once again the Kogon's sinister snake noise filled the piazza. "The dumbman prithonerth have brought their leader with them. He thpeakth to me. Thee!"

The bodyguard stood back a little and Jinsha emerged on to the balcony carrying a long spear. Spiked on the top, its long, thin hair waving gently over its black and sunken cheeks, was the smoked, hollow-eyed head of Timur.

The Kogon were too astounded to make a sound. "Thith ith the Malik of the Grothny Thedth," explained Xsani. "A living-dead dumbman." She paused. "My friend."

The crowd, struggling to take in what they saw and heard, remained completely silent. "Now," Xsani went on, "bring in the Grothny!"

At her command, Tarangala and Yalisha unlocked the sty where Jamshid and Giv were held and led them out. Still under the influence of the leaves, they stumbled and stared wildly about them.

"Grothny!" cried Xsani. "What do you thee here?"

The two men looked up at the balcony. "Timur!" they gasped in unison. "Malik Timur!"

On orders from the Malika, they were guided to the front of the balcony and told to kneel before the head of their leader. The posture was another idea Xsani had picked up from the strange images on the walls of her headquarters.

"Repeat after me," she said quietly but firmly. "Mighty Timur…"

"Mighty Timur."

"Who livth for ever…"

"Who livth – er, lives – for ever."

"You and the Malika are one."

"You and the Mailka are one."

This done, Xsani went through the same process with the entire Kogon tribe. It was strange, she thought, how reassuring chanted repetitions were.

The ceremony concluded with Jamshid and Giv telling the company how they would obey Timur and follow Malika Xsani as the Kogon did. As she lay down beside her young kumfort that night, the leader of the elusive Fairy-Zeds smiled to herself in the darkness. So far, it had all gone better than she had expected. Further progress depended on Jamshid and Giv. After this evening's performance, she was sure they would not fail her.

It was several moons since Timur had left the Grozny and set off for Alba in a desperate attempt to get hold of the Soterion. His tribe had never been left leaderless for so long. Not only was their Malik absent, but his two Captains, Jumshid and Jamshid, had gone too. Navid had slain Jumshid as he tried to prevent the Constant mission from crossing the deadly River No-Man; Jamshid, like his master, had simply disappeared.

Kamal had been left in temporary command of the tribe. He was a scrawny, skull-faced man of seventeen winters with an ulcerous sore where his right hand had once been. His disposition was ugly, even for a Zed. From his master he had learned cruelty but not subtlety. For the first moon, this did not matter much. He sent out pillaging parties to bring in food, regulated access to the breeding slaves and punished with exemplary viciousness anyone questioning his authority.

But by the second moon his men had grown restless. The Grozny flourished by plundering Constant settlements for their food and women. Camped beside the No-Man for days on end, they laid waste to the countryside far around. The men grew hungry and bored. Insubordination crept in. Kamal responded with still harsher punishment, and on the swampy banks of the slime-green stream resentment festered like a disease.

It came to a head one morning when Gawlip, a broken-nosed warrior of sixteen winters, was arrested for abusing one of the female prisoners. These Constant women were needed to maintain the tribe's population, but it was long accepted, even among the most uncouth, that a mother with a child of two winters or less was not to be touched. Timur punished those who broke this rule with a whipping and, sometimes, the removal of a few teeth. Kamal went further and ordered that Gawlip be flung into the No-Man. It was a capital punishment – as the river's name made clear, no one entering that sulphurous swamp ever came out alive. If by some miracle they avoided the ravenous crocodiles, they fell victim to the lethal water-snakes.

When Kamal gave his order, the accused was lying on

the grass at his master's feet. Noticing that no one had come forward to carry out his instructions, Kamal looked up angrily. His expression froze. At least half the tribe had formed a furious circle round him.

Quietly at first, they began the deadly chant: "Zed blood! Zed blood! Kill! Kill! Kill! Zed blood! Zed blood! Kill! Kill! Kill!"

With each repetition, the circle closed in around the doomed leader. It was no more than three paces from him when the chanting was interrupted by a tremendous roar. "Timur say no!" rolled down like thunder from the crest of the bank.

Startled, the Grozny looked up to see who or what dared to take the name of their leader in vain. It was Jamshid. Beside him, looking rather less imposing, stood Giv. Behind the ridge, out of sight of the Grozny, Zektiv Yalisha and six Kogon warriors crouched in the undergrowth to observe what went on. They were under strict instructions to kill Jamshid and Giv immediately if they showed any sign of deviating from Xsani's instructions.

Kamal was the first to respond. "Jamshid? You back?"

"Back and mighty, Kamal!" boomed the Captain. "With Giv." His companion nodded eagerly.

"Where, er, where Timur?" asked Kamal anxiously.

"With me," replied Jamshid, who had been preparing his responses ever since leaving the Kogon camp. "Timur live with me. Timur speak with me. Timur come again!"

The quicker-witted of the Grozny warriors began to chant. "Ti-mur! Ti-mur! Ti-mur!" Before long the whole tribe joined in until the air rang with the name of their former Malik. Above them Jamshid and Giv looked at each other in silent satisfaction.

The rest of the task was swiftly accomplished. Jamshid explained how Timur, now an Over-Malik (a phrase of Xsani's invention), had appointed him the new Malik of the Grozny. Kamal joined Giv as one of his two Captains. What really won the tribe over was the promise of action. Jamshid would lead them to his new friends and reunion with Timur. After that, there would be fighting and bloodshed aplenty in an attack on the Constants of Alba.

No mention was made of the Kogon, nor of Yalisha and her hidden posse of wardens. Xsani had decided, quite rightly, that the Grozny could manage just one new piece of information at a time. The elevation of Timur to Over-Malik and his replacement at the head of the tribe by Jamshid was enough for the moment. The announcement of friendship, or at least an alliance with flabtoads, would be too much for a Zed brain to assimilate in one go. It could wait.

The migration of the Grozny to the site chosen by Yalisha was soon accomplished. Camped roughly ten thousand paces distant from the Kogon base at Filna, they passed their days happily raiding a small Constant settlement nearby and waiting for further instructions. Jamshid loved his new role. He returned from one of the raids bearing a huge fur coat and matching hat that he insisted on wearing day and night. He also demanded to be addressed as 'Grand Malik Jamshid', even by Giv. "Because," he boasted, "Jamshid speaks with Timur."

Giv, though happy to be with the Grozny and their familiar

ways, was unsure about the grand airs his new leader was adopting. Whenever he saw Jamshid strutting around the camp in his furs, he couldn't help remembering how Malika Xsani had humiliated him when they first met and how he had fawned before her.

Xsani! There was a leader indeed, Giv told himself. The poise, the elegant blue robe, the bob of fair hair – yes, he missed her! His heart – if indeed he had one – jumped therefore when he was woken one night by Jinsha whispering in his ear.

"Shh! Not a sound." She had an important message for Jamshid and him. Timur, the Over-Malik, wanted to see them again. Tomorrow night he demanded to speak with ten Grozny leaders.

"Ten?" Giv struggled to remember what it meant.

Jinsha held her upraised hands before his face. "All fingers, dumbman," she hissed. "Come to where the sun goes down and I will lead you to the Malika."

"Sun go down," echoed Giv.

"Yes. And ten only. If you fail your Timur, you die!" With that, she vanished into the night.

The next morning, when the two of them were alone, Giv passed on the message to Jamshid. At first the Grand Malik was suspicious, asking why Timur had not spoken to him directly. Giv decided that it was because Jamshid had been with a breeding slave and not easily approached. He nodded and rolled his shoulders in a self-important manner. Even so, he thought, it would have been good if the Over-Malik Timur had addressed him personally. Maybe he would soon, perhaps even at tonight's meeting…

The Grozny party set off at sunset. They took a twisting trail through the woods for about five thousand paces until Jamshid, who insisted on leading, found his way barred by a rope tied across the path. At the same time, a low hissing started up in the surrounding shadows. Remembering the last time they had been ambushed, Jamshid and Giv froze; Kamal and the other Grozny swore loudly and gripped their weapons tightly, preparing for battle. When Jinsha's voice floated out of the darkness, one or two of them started forward to find the speaker. Jamshid called them back angrily.

Jinsha, well hidden in the trees, announced herself as Timur's messenger. She would guide them to their Over-Malik. They must leave their weapons beside the path, where they would be guarded until their return, and follow her in silence.

"Good flabtoad," explained Jamshid in a hoarse whisper. "Friend of Timur. Obey and follow."

On reaching Filna, the delegation was led straight to the sty where a fresh basket of smoke leaves had been prepared. While the smoke was working its magic, the Kogon assembled in the piazza. Inside Xsani's headquarters Timur's head was skewered to its spike. At midnight, as a full moon hung like a huge and cruel parody of the former Malik, the Grozny were released. Like children who had just mastered the art of walking, they weaved their way unsteadily towards the balcony.

When all was ready, torch bearers emerged, followed by Xsani and her gleaming bodyguard and, finally, the elevated head of Timur.

"Look!" called Jamshid, pointing eagerly up at the grisly icon. "Jamshid tell you true! Timur come! Timur come!"

Without prompting, the crowd started the slow, rolling chant of "Ti-mur! Ti-mur! Ti-mur!" Jamshid was staring hard at the blackened head. Its ghoulish features, flecked with orange firelight, were even more awe-inspiring than he remembered them. Transported with wonder, he gazed up at the moon, then back at the head. Feeling dizzy, he grasped the stone balustrade to steady himself.

Timur was here ... Timur was with him ... Wait! Timur was speaking to him!

Without warning, the Grand Malik scrambled urgently to the top of the balustrade. The bodyguard swiftly stepped forward to protect their leader. Jamshid shook his head and waved them aside.

"No, no!" he cried. "Hear Jamshid! Hear Jamshid!" He turned to face the piazza. "Timur speak me! Command me! He go Alba – now I go Alba! Grand Malik Jamshid attack Alba! Attack Alba!"

As he finished, the piazza filled with hissing and the grinning Grozny jostled each other in eager anticipation. Most of them didn't know what Alba was, but the thought of any attack sent them into paroxysms of delight.

Xsani felt the situation sliding out of her control. She couldn't have this idiot jumping up like that and claiming to speak for Timur. That was her role. She walked quickly to the front of the balcony and called for silence.

"Jamthid ith right," she said. "Timur told me the dumbman

thould lead a party of Grothny againtht Alba. It will prepare for the main attack. I will lead that. But Jamthid's part ith tho, tho important, thaid Timur. He leadth, we follow. Timur thaid tho."

The situation was rescued. Jamshid, flattered to think Timur had given him the role of trailblazer, accepted Xsani's guidance. He returned to his people and told them he would lead a band of twenty-five warriors against Alba the next day. When they had captured and sacked the settlement, Malika Xsani and Timur could enter in triumph. The Grozny roared their support.

Back in Filna, Xsani explained her thinking to Jinsha, Tarangala and Yalisha. If Jamshid succeeded, which was almost inconceivable, he would have done their work for them. His failure, on the other hand, would mean the loss of only twenty-five warriors and get the lumbering fool out of their way. The plan, particularly the latter part of it, met with unqualified approval.

Shortly after dawn on a grey drizzly morning, Sakamir's small party slipped out of the gate near the fire stone and headed for the arid region between the desert and the forest. They moved with extreme caution. Sakamir took the lead, then Potr, with Sammy and Jannat at the rear. Patrols normally went in a broad arc that brought them back to the gate above the Soterion. By sunhigh, when it was clear they were not following this route but heading out deeper into unknown territory, Jannat asked the leader where they were headed.

"Where I take you," came the curt reply.

Sammy was not impressed. "So where's that then, Sakamir?"

To get her to come clean about the purpose of their mission, he added, "We goin' hunting or what?"

She looked at him coldly, wondering how much he knew. "Alright," she said eventually. "I'll tell you. Timur's tribe, the Grozny, are believed to be still in this region. I think you know our evidence for that, Sammy."

"Yeah. I found it."

"Good. Well, they've probably got something we'd rather they didn't have. Our job is to seize it. So our first task is simple," she concluded. "Find the Grozny."

Sammy exchanged quizzical looks with Jannat. He didn't like the situation one bit. Although Sakamir had confirmed the purpose of the patrol, he still didn't understand why she had chosen to lead it. Of course, she might really share Cyrus' anxiety about how Timur's head might inspire a Grozny revenge attack. But if she didn't, then why was she so keen to find them? And why had she brought Potr with her? A short, meagre man of sixteen winters, he was renowned for his feeble physique and lack of courage – hardly the sort of warrior to have at one's side in an emergency. Yes, Sammy concluded, I must take great care where I put my feet.

The small band moved cautiously in the direction Timur was believed to have come from. Cyrus had worked out the route by studying a map in the Soterion collection. Every half day or so, the patrol climbed the highest point they could find and studied the landscape for signs of movement. Towards the end of the third day, their patience was rewarded.

As they stood in a clump of trees on a low, sandy ridge, they became aware of a loud noise approaching in front of them. They ducked down out of sight and listened. Jannat, who had experienced a situation like this several years before, reckoned the sound was being made by some two dozen men. Its nature – part chant, part song – could mean only one thing. Zeds.

Keeping the enemy to their right, the patrol shadowed the Zeds until they stopped for the night. They believed themselves far from any human threat and posted no sentries. When all was quiet, Sakamir sent Potr and Jannat forward to learn what they could. They returned not long afterwards with astonishing news.

The band was indeed about twenty strong. They were Grozny Zeds and, incredibly, they appeared to be on their way to attack Alba.

Sammy blew silently through his lips. "Well, well, Sakamir," he asked quietly. "There's your Grozny. So what does we do next?"

5

The Burden of Loneliness

"I'll tell you exactly what we're going to do, Sammy," said Sakamir in a brisk half-whisper. "You and Jannat are going back to Alba as swiftly as you can to warn them. Potr and I will recce further to find out what's happening."

A look of concern crossed Jannat's face. "Are you sure you'll be safe, Sakamir? I mean, just two of you out here…"

"Thank you, Jannat, but Potr and I will be fine. You and Sammy will be on your own, too, don't forget." Sakamir's tone was brusque and decisive – it was clear the matter was not open for discussion. Jannat, raised to obey orders instinctively, got ready to leave.

Unquestioning obedience did not come so readily to Sammy. "So you'll go on looking for this thing what the Grozny shouldn't have?" he asked.

He was shaken by the ferocity of Sakamir's reply. "What I do or do not do, Sammy, is none of your business. This is my patrol and it does what I say, got it?"

No one had addressed Sammy like this since the days of his childhood in the Children of Gova community, and he didn't like it. "Yeah, but you don't have to go talkin' to me –"

Sakamir's hand slid towards the knife at her side. Seeing it, Jannat took Sammy firmly by the arm and pulled him away. "Come on, Sammy! No arguing. We've got to return to Alba right now. Duty, remember? Let's go!"

Reluctantly, Sammy allowed himself to be led off and, without a word of farewell, Jannat and he headed off into the night. They walked in silence for a while, pausing only to check their direction from the stars. Eventually, when they were sure they had put sufficient distance between the Grozny and themselves, they stopped to rest and get some sleep.

"Thanks Jannat," said Sammy a little sheepishly as they lay down on a patch of dry sand beneath overhanging foliage. "Got a bit carried away with Sakamir, didn't I?"

"Just a bit, yes."

"But she's a nasty piece of work, isn't she?"

Jannat yawned. "Yes, she is. And I wish I knew what she's up to."

"So do I. And I feel sorry for that Potr bloke. He don't stand a chance, do he?"

Sammy and Jannat made it back to Alba in less than a day. The return of just two members of the patrol caused a bit of a stir, although Yash seemed less worried than most. He said he had full confidence in his copemate and was sure she had a good reason for wanting to continue in the field. "Obviously she wants to find out what's going on, doesn't she? It's her duty."

Sammy nodded. He wondered how much Yash really knew.

Seeing he had agreement, Yash relaxed further. "I've never heard of Zeds dividing their forces before, so we need to know what these Grozny barbarians are up to."

Sammy nodded a second time.

"Good. So I'll give Sakamir and Potr another four or five days. If they haven't shown up after that, then we might start worrying. Meanwhile, we've got this warband to deal with, right? Tell us about it, Jannat. All you know."

As soon as Jannat had finished, she and Sammy went off to get some rest and Yash called a meeting with Bahm, his senior Konnel, and Cyrus, the only Constant with first-hand knowledge of Grozny tactics.

A Zed attack, however minor, could not be taken lightly, and the Emir was in his element. "Step one," he said crisply, curling his right hand round the forefinger of the left, "is to send out a scout group. They'll find the enemy and work out when they're likely to reach our territory."

He opened his palm and grasped the index finger as well. "For step two we have a choice. Either we set up an ambush away from Alba, or we trap them up against the walls. Thoughts?"

Bahm wanted to pin the Zeds against the walls. "It's the obvious tactic," agreed Cyrus, "but if –"

"No ifs," cut in Yash. "I agree it's the obvious thing to do, so we'll do it. Bahm, you take command of the ambush party."

Cyrus took a deep breath to calm himself. Once again he was

infuriated by Yash's high-handed behaviour – why invite him to the meeting if everything he said was ignored?

Shortly before sundown, the Emir's scout group returned with strange news. Yash summoned Bahm and Cyrus again to hear the report. The Grozny, they were told, were just twenty-five strong, as Jannat had said. What's more, they were making no effort at concealment. Instead, they were advancing in broad daylight, chanting some sort of slogan.

"It's like they reckon they're invisible," the patrol commander said, shaking his head in bewilderment.

"Invincible, eh?" grunted Bahm. "We'll see 'bout that."

Cyrus asked about the chant. It was difficult to make out all the words, the commander explained, but what sounded like 'Malik Timur' and 'head' were often repeated.

Yash looked away hurriedly. "Cyrus has a theory about Timur's head," he said, turning to Bahm with a condescending smile. "Personally, I think it's nonsense."

Cyrus ground his teeth but said nothing.

"Anyway," Yash went on, "what these Zeds are saying doesn't matter. They'll be here tomorrow morning, that's all we need to know. Take your archers out tonight, Bahm – around a hundred should be enough – and divide them in two, fifty on each flank. As the Zeds approach the walls, close in behind them. I'll shoot an arrow into the sky as a signal for you to attack. Got it?"

"Got it."

Cyrus did not. On four or five previous occasions he had held back from challenging Yash's decisions, but not this time. As lives were at stake, he felt it his duty to offer a word of caution. "Shouldn't we check to make sure there isn't a larger force behind the small one?" he suggested. "That's the sort of trick Timur would have used – ambush the ambushers."

Yash shook his head vigorously. "Come off it, Cyrus!" he laughed. "You and your daft ideas! First the head business, now this. What do you say, Bahm?"

"Never heard of a Zed dreaming up anything half as clever as that. No, I say we go ahead as planned."

"So do I," echoed Yash.

Cyrus gave it one more try. "But the commander said the chant mentioned Timur and his head. If that's true, their new leader must be pretty clever to understand the power of a head –"

"Who said it was definitely 'head'?" interrupted Yash. "More likely to be 'dead'. Those useless Grozny are probably on some suicide mission now their leader's gone."

"And we'll make sure the suicide bit of the mission is successful, eh?" chuckled Bahm. Yash joined in with his friend's laughter.

Seeing there was no point in pursuing the point further, Cyrus went off to find Sammy and reunite him with Corby. At least one thing was clear, he told himself. Whatever Yash said, he was pretty sure the Grozny had Timur's head and their new leader was using it to inspire them. He clenched his fists in frustration. If Yash had done what he suggested at the beginning and burned Timur's body, none of this would be happening. Emir or not, the man was infuriating! And maybe dangerous, too. Wasn't it strange how little concern he'd shown over his copemate's failure to return? Maybe he didn't want her back?

There was a lot he didn't know. Trying to make sense of what was going on was like attempting to read a book with half the words missing. The way things were turning out was so disappointing. Roxanne and he had hoped the Soterion would bring relief and happiness, not confusion and mistrust. How perceptive had Padmar's dying warning been!

Sammy wasn't able to tell Cyrus much he didn't already know and, after agreeing to join his friend in the ambush force setting off that evening, the young man returned to his dormitory to catch up on lost sleep. Cyrus got round Yash's inevitable veto on their joining up by going to Bahm directly. Without hesitation, the bluff Konnel agreed to Cyrus and Sammy being part of his force. Hardly a surprise, thought Cyrus. I reckon he'd be relieved if neither Sammy nor I made it back inside the walls alive.

The battle that took place the following morning was one of the easiest and most decisive in all Alba's history. In fact, it was more of a massacre than a true battle. As expected, the Zeds neared the settlement not long after dawn. Their chanting was audible long before they came into view, and this time the words were clear: "Malik Timur he not dead! He led Grozny with his head!"

"Told you," whispered Cyrus to Sammy, who was crouched by his side with a hand on Corby's collar. They were about forty paces from the nearest Zeds as they swaggered by. "They cut off the head and they're using it. But I haven't seen it, have you?"

"No. Sakamir didn't say she'd seen it, neither."

Once out of the woods, Jamshid brought his band to a halt. Realising a frontal assault on the moss-covered concrete walls was impossible, he moved left and made for the small Patrol Gate. Behind them, the shadowing force of Albans advanced to the fringe of the trees.

Moments later, a single arrow rose into the air above the walls. One of the Zeds saw it and pointed at it with a rusty pike. It was his last gesture. Even before Yash's arrow hit the ground, dozens of others were speeding towards the unprotected barbarians. The majority struck home, piercing thighs, backs, necks and shoulders with dreadful thuds.

Half the Grozny fell at once, some killed outright, others yelling in pain and savage fury as they tried to pluck the barbs from their bleeding flesh. Immediately, the Albans rushed from their cover to finish them off with axe and sword.

Jamshid, at the head of his force and furthest from the rain of arrows, had remained unharmed. When he saw what had happened, he froze in astonishment before running back towards the safety of the woods.

Cyrus and Sammy had hurried forward with the others as the arrows fell. One thrust of Cyrus' spear ended the agonised writhing of a Zed trying to pull an arrow from his throat. Corby pinned another to the ground while Sammy dispatched him with his new sword, a present from Jannat.

Cyrus was going over to congratulate his young friend, when he noticed an odd-looking Zed in a fur hat sprinting for the trees to his right. "No you don't!" he muttered, and set off in pursuit.

Sensing someone was on his tail and closing fast, Jamshid stopped and turned to face his pursuer. Cyrus raised his spear. The Zed saw he was trapped and, in a gesture of wild desperation, flung his gut-ripper in the general direction of his pursuer. It missed by a good five feet, and Cyrus closed in for the kill.

Now unarmed, Jamshid turned and ran for his life, expecting a spear to bury itself between his shoulder blades at any moment. It never came. As Cyrus was on the point of launching his missile, he was distracted by a cry behind him. Sammy! He glanced round to see that the gut-ripper had skidded off the stony ground and rebounded against Sammy's leg. No bone was broken, but blood was flowing from a gash two fingers long below his left knee.

By the time Cyrus turned to face his opponent, the fur-clad Zed had disappeared into the forest. Corby whined pitifully, unsure whether to stay to look after his new master or chase after the man who had harmed him. His protective instincts got the better of him and, sitting beside Sammy, he licked at the tears of pain running down the young man's face.

Sammy was the Albans' only injury. Later that morning, twenty-four slain Zeds were carried to the ravine and hurled into the abyss. Bahm, the operation's leader, was hailed as a hero, and Yash overlooked Cyrus' participation in the fight. No one was blamed for the escape of a single enemy, although Cyrus was angry with himself for not having finished off the strange-looking creature when he had the opportunity.

More galling was the teasing he had to endure. So there might be a larger force of Zeds behind the smaller one, might there? Bahm mocked, only half in jest. And what about this Timur head business? asked Yash. It was supposed to inspire them, wasn't that what Cyrus had said? Well, it hadn't done them much good, had it? They'd even forgotten to bring it with them!

Cyrus kept his anger to himself. They might laugh at him now, but one day he'd be proved right. The head was still out there. Moreover, he was certain the blundering fools who'd wandered into Bahm's ambush did not control the totem. They were typical brainless Zeds. Someone, somewhere – a leader of unusual insight and subtlety – had sent them. But why? Surely not simply to avenge Timur's death? No. This unseen commander was using the head to further their own ambitions. And as these ambitions involved Alba, they must also involve the Soterion.

Cyrus gave a slight shudder. He was essentially a straightforward person who liked direct paths and clear-cut decisions. Uncertainty troubled him. In the end, he decided that he'd settle nothing by worrying about it and hurried off to attend to the practical matter of Sammy's wound.

Fortunately for Sakamir and Potr, Xsani's Eyes spotted them before the Grozny. The lookouts rounded up the pair in the customary manner and brought them before their Malika. That first meeting was a thrilling encounter. Two highly intelligent, extremely ambitious women circling each other like wild beasts, each fascinated by the creature before them. They both realised they would be stronger together, but neither trusted the other. Why was Sakamir here? the Makila asked.

She wanted to join the Zeds. She would lead them to save the Soterion.

The Soterion? Xsani had heard of this and wanted to know more.

Sakamir gave a brief outline of the contents of the secret vault, its books and how they contained all the knowledge and wisdom of the Long Dead.

Did they mention a dumbman in a round yellow hat? asked Xsani.

No, Sakamir had never heard of such a person. But she did know that somewhere within that library lay details of the Salvation Project. The Malika hadn't heard of the Salvation Project? Well, it was something the Long Dead had been working on as they died out. It would abolish the Death Month and allow people to live way beyond their eighteenth winter, as they used to. Perhaps even seeing one hundred winters.

Xsani was impressed. And this Soterion, so full of powerful information and ideas, was that what Timur had been after?

Yes. And a Constant named Cyrus, who could read, was working on it. Sakamir said he was well-meaning but stupid. He would fail.

Why?

Because all Constants were stupid. Sakimir's copemate –

Her what?

Friend, companion, breeding partner, Sakamir clarified. Did the Kogon have a different name?

They did. 'Kumforts'. It had nothing to do with breeding.

Sakamir liked that idea. She explained how the Constants of Alba, led by the conservative Bahm, were getting fed up with Cyrus. She was afraid that before long they would throw him out and destroy the Soterion. With it would go all chance of long life and power…

Xsani's interest was growing. Could Sakamir read?

She was learning, she replied. So when the Zeds took over Alba with the help of her copemate, she would then destroy him, capture the Soterion and pass on its information to Xsani …

Xsani did not like the sound of that. If they were to work together, it had to be on an equal footing. Sakamir had to teach Xsani to read.

Alright, she would. And she would become a Zed.

And accept a Z tattoo?

Of course.

When that was done, the Malika concluded, they could progress.

Sakamir refused to be held down for her tattooing. She even kept her eyes open as the red-hot Z sizzled against her forehead and her nose filled with the stench of her own burning flesh.

"Imprethive," said Xsani, standing directly in front of the new arrival and observing her closely. "You are one of uth now."

Sakamir angrily brushed away the tears of pain that ran down her thin cheeks. "I'm glad. You and I will make a powerful partnership, Xsani."

The Malika gave no direct response. Instead, she unsheathed a knife hanging at Jinsha's waist and held it, handle first, for Sakamir to grasp. "If you are a Thed," she said with a smile, "you mutht hate Conthanth, yeth?"

"Yes, I do. They're feeble. Pathetic."

"Pathetic, yeth. There ith one of thethe pathetic creaturth bethide you. A dumbman, too." She pointed the knife handle towards the dismal figure of Potr, bound hand and foot and bleeding from the several wounds he had received during his capture. "Thutch a puny thing could never be a breeding thlave, tho he ith of no uthe to uth. Kill him."

Sakamir took the knife and, pausing only to decide where best to strike, plunged it upwards into Potr's heart from beneath his ribs. For an instant, he stood transfixed, his eyes staring in horrified disbelief, before crumpling to the floor. Sakamir stooped, pulled the knife from the body, wiped it on her filthy tunic and handed it back to Jinsha.

"And now?" she said, turning to Xsani. For the first time in her adult life, the glee in her eyes matched the smile on her lips.

"And now," replied Xsani enigmatically, "And now we can progreth."

As Xsani lay in bed waiting for dawn, she reflected upon recent events. It was strange, she thought, how for so long day had followed day, moon had followed moon in the same cycle of watching and moving and fighting. Then, without warning, everything had changed. The usual patterns were broken. Customs and practices that had served the tribe for generations had been set aside. In this new world, her task was not simply to preserve, as previous Malikas had done, but to lead. Something momentous was happening, she was sure of it, and she had to be at the very centre. In control.

It all revolved around this Soterion. Having heard the

explanation of the turncoat Sakamir – if the woman was telling the truth, of course – she understood why it was so important. No wonder Timur had wanted to get hold of it! Living for one hundred winters – that was for ever! She wondered, in a lighter moment, whether her friend in the round yellow hat had lived so long.

But it was not just a matter of length of life, but of power and glory. Once she had the Soterion, the might of the Long Dead would be hers. The skill that had constructed these buildings and fashioned those brilliant objects that lay rusting or broken, all that would be at her command. The Long Dead must have used weapons as well, or how else could they have defeated their enemies? Such awful majesty for her alone!

She already had the Grozny under her rule. Now she had this renegade Constant, who promised to open Alba's gates to her and her allies. Sakamir and her idiotic kumfort – 'copemate Yash' she had called him – would see to that. Apparently Yash had believed Sakamir when she told him that together, with Zed help, they would seize the Soterion. Together! Pah! What dolts these dumbmans were!

Sakamir was in league with the Kogon. She had been tattooed, so there was no turning back. But in the end it didn't matter – she would be killed as soon as they were inside Alba and she was no longer useful. Two could play the betrayal game, couldn't they?

Seeing a watery light seep through the broken windows of her headquarters, Xsani shook Jinsha awake. "Come, my kumfort," she said, smoothing down the young woman's hair, "there ith tho much to do. You and I mutht learn to read, muthn't we? And maybe we thould do ath Thakamir thayth and find thome more allieth."

Jinsha yawned. "More dumbmans, Malika?"

"Perhapth. We could uthe my thaddow, Giv."

Her kumfort groaned. "But he's so gormless, Malika!"

Xsani smiled. "Yeth, I know. But thometimeth it taketh a thtupid perthon to catch a thtupid perthon, Jintha. Bethideth, Giv adoreth me, and I like that."

"But don't I adore you, Malika?" said Jinsha, sliding closer to her mistress.

"Of courth. But thath different, ithn't it?"

The Constants possessed only half-remembered fragments of Long Dead medical knowledge. The link between dirt and disease was generally understood, but not the bacteriology behind it. Remembering how Zavar had died of his wounds early in the Mission, Cyrus had spent ages searching the Soterion library for a text that explained how his friend's death might have been prevented. He found what he was looking for by accident. Moving a book entitled *First World War* – which meant nothing to him – he came across a thin, brightly coloured pamphlet entitled *First Aid and Basic Medicine: What Every Parent Needs to Know*. The individual words just about made sense, but together … what was 'first aid'? He soon learned, and rapidly gained a fair grasp of the subject.

Treating Sammy's wound was the first time Long Dead information was put to practical use. The gash was deep and long. The traditional Constant treatment for such injuries was to wash them in water and bind them up, perhaps with some herb or other laid over the incision. The results were, at best, uncertain. While some made a complete recovery, many died of septicaemia, as Zavar had done. Following the instructions in his pamphlet, Cyrus did things differently. He cleaned the wound thoroughly with boiled water before stitching it with a needle he had held over a flame. To his relief and delight, the cut healed cleanly and Sammy was walking comfortably within a few days.

In normal times, such a rapid recovery would have been a major talking point among Albans. But these were far from normal times. Despite Bahm's ambush victory, or because of it, an air of unease hung over the community. Everyone knew what lay behind it, though only Bahm and his colleagues spoke of it openly. The Soterion.

As Bahm never tired of telling people, since the opening of that wretched vault there had been more trouble than anyone could remember. An Emir had been murdered and his replacement executed for treason; Alba had been temporarily controlled by a Zed; the copemate of the new Emir had disappeared and was probably dead; Zeds were making direct attacks on the settlement; and every day a stranger took off some of the most able members of the community, including the Emir, in order to teach them how to read books that would allow them to live for ever.

It was pernicious nonsense! What was wrong with living for eighteen winters before slipping off quickly like everyone else? The Death Month was bad enough without stretching it out for years and years. How horrible it'd be to grow old slowly, gradually getting feebler and feebler and of no use to anyone. Anyway, living for ever hadn't done the Long Dead any good, had it, despite all their clever technology? Where were they now? Gone!

No, growled Bahm, the old Constant ways were best. With them, everyone knew where they were and everything had its place. Cyrus and his Soterion were nothing but trouble.

Such talk wouldn't have mattered much if Yash had had a firm grip on the situation. To Cyrus' dismay, the Emir seemed hardly to notice the grumbling. He didn't agree with it, Cyrus was sure, because he came regularly to the classes and was making steady if slow progress with his reading and writing. It was as if Yash tolerated Bahm's comments because they undermined Cyrus.

Seven days after Bahm's victory over the Zeds, the breach between Cyrus and Yash widened still further. It had rained all night and was still drizzling the next morning when the two met as they sheltered beneath the wall next to the patrol gate.

"No news of Sakamir, I suppose?" asked Cyrus.

Yash looked at him suspiciously. "No. Why?"

"Well, I'm concerned, Yash. She's been gone a while."

"I've been told she talked to you before she went, Cyrus. Is that true?"

The remark caught Cyrus by surprise. Yash had previously shown little concern over his missing copemate, so what was he driving at now? "We did have a few words, yes."

"About what?"

"About the Grozny Zeds. She asked about their tactics and so on. Because of Timur, she thought there might still be a few remaining in the area and she wanted to be prepared." That's all true, thought Cyrus. There was no need to mention the head.

Yash's tone switched from sombre to aggressive. "You know, if she doesn't come back I'll hold you partly responsible."

"Me?"

"Yes, you, Cyrus. You and your daft talk of Timur's head. You may have killed my dearest copemate, I hope you realise that." So saying, Yash stomped off into the rain, leaving Cyrus wondering what had got into the man.

Events in that afternoon's class added to his confusion. Yash normally positioned himself on Cyrus' left, apart from the other students. Today, he made a point of sitting next to Miouda. He joked with her, asked her for help and placed his cheek alongside hers as he leaned over to read what she had written. When the class broke up, he put an arm round her shoulders and said he looked forward to working with her again tomorrow.

Miouda was clearly annoyed and hung around on her own as the others left.

"I'm sorry," Cyrus said when they were alone.

"You saw it?"

"Of course. It made me angry."

"Me too. It spoils everything."

"Everything?"

She lifted her clear blue eyes and smiled. "No, not everything, Cyrus. I really like what we're doing. It's as if I've been lifted up by a giant bird and dropped into a brighter, better world."

He moved closer and took her hand. "Reckon your bird is strong enough to pick up two people, Miouda?"

"Why not? It must be hard trying to do everything on your own."

Though very simple words, they did much to ease the burden of his loneliness.

After his brief meeting with Miouda, Cyrus went for a walk around the settlement. The rain had left the air heavy and humid. Without thinking where he was going, he wandered up the hill to the square before proceeding towards the main gate. It was quite dark and he could just make out the silhouettes of two figures up on the wall ahead of him. As he watched, one of them approached the other and appeared to grab hold of them. There was a muffled shout. The second figure pulled away and ran down the steps into the road.

Standing in the shadows, Cyrus was invisible to the figure hurrying by. But he saw clearly enough who it was. Jannat. He waited to see who her molester was. He planned to give them a piece of his mind. As the second figure descended the steps into the road, Cyrus recognised Yash immediately.

Twice in one day? What was the man up to? Only that morning he had been bemoaning the loss of his 'dearest copemate'. Insincere bully! Cyrus' anger, which he had been fighting to keep under control for some time, finally got the better of him. He stepped out into the road.

"That's Zed behaviour, Yash!" The two men were barely a pace apart.

"Well, look who's slithering about in the dark to spy on people!" drawled Yash. "Mind your own business, Outsider!"

With difficulty, Cyrus stopped himself from punching him. "Bullying is everyone's business," he warned, realising he had to leave before things got out of control. "So, Emir or not, cut it out!" He turned on his heel and, seething with fury, hurried back to the Ghasar.

The Emir's retaliation was quick and cruel. Entering the Ghasar shortly before sunhigh the following day, Cyrus found Bahm and five of his friends already there.

"What's going on?" Cyrus asked.

"You'll be seeing soon enough," said Bahm calmly. When Yash entered, he stood arrogantly aside. The rest of the class came in and gathered round Cyrus.

"Noticed summat?" asked Bahm, looking hard at Cyrus.

Cyrus looked around. "Yes. The class has grown in number – and one of our students is missing. As well as Sakamir, of course."

"Don't you try to be clever, Cyrus," said Bahm. "We all know Sakamir's child, young Jalus, is missing. And we knows why."

"Why?"

"'Cos he's sick. Sick of study and being stuck indoors. They say he's going to die. Certain. This Soterion thing has ruined 'im, like it's ruining all the rest of us.

"Listen, Cyrus. It's got to stop. All them books has got to go back in that there vault and the key thrown away. It's the only answer. The Emir agrees, don't you Yash?"

"Er, yes. Though it'd be better if I kept the key, Bahm. You never know –"

Cyrus had had enough. "Yes, we do know, Yash! We have it in our power to lift ourselves out of our nasty, brutish and short lives, and enter a new world where children do not die from the slightest illness, where people live in comfort and peace in a Zed-free world. And you – yes, all of you standing there with Bahm – you want to turn that down? Think what you are saying! Use your imaginations!"

Straight away, several of Cyrus' pupils spoke in his support. One of the mentors who helped the younger ones said that though he was only just getting the hang of reading, he had already learned incredible things. The Long Dead had flying machines called aeroplanes… And they could cut people open and take out sick bits of their bodies, added one of the twelve-year-olds.

Miouda spoke last. Looking directly at her Emir, she said, "And you, Yash, our leader – you appreciate the wonder of this place. I have heard you catch your breath at what you're reading, and I have heard you long for the day when we find the Salvation Project. I'm right, aren't I?"

Bahm frowned. "Well, Emir?"

Before he could speak, a wiry young man with a slight limp walked purposefully to the front. "Hang on a bit! Excuse me, Emir, but we're all getting a bit het up over this, aren't we? I reckon Mister Bahm and his lot can't see no point in all this book learning stuff, right?"

"Too right!" rumbled Bahm.

"Ok. What you need is what the Long Dead called proof. I

read about it. You need someone to show you that we're doing good, helping everyone. Agreed, Bahm? Yash?"

The two men nodded.

"Ok. So what I say is this. Mister Cyrus has read amazing things. He learned from these books how to make my leg better when it was cut bad. Now this is what he's goin' to do..."

Sammy paused and looked around at his audience's shocked, expectant faces. "He's going to make that Jalus better. 'Cure' him, as the Long Dead put it. If he can't do it, we'll do what Bahm says and lock all the books up again. But if he does cure little Jalus, no more arguing and squabbling, ok?"

A general murmur of agreement filled the hall. All eyes turned to Yash. "Alright," he said, looking across at Cyrus. "A fair challenge. We've wasted enough time on letters and reading and all that. Prove the Soterion's actually useful – or we'll lock everything back in the vault and forget it. And our visitors can go back to where they came from, too."

6

The Coalition

Constant and Zed had divided before the last corpse of the Great Death began to rot. Ever since, while Constants tried to preserve the Long Dead's ways and values, Zeds did their best to wipe them out. They didn't know the meaning of mercy. Constants did, but couldn't imagine straining its qualities as far as a Zed. Not surprisingly, all relations between the two were bloody.

All relations? Not quite. The seductive power of the Soterion had changed everything. It had spawned a new and surprising partnership – if that is the right word – between the Constant Sakamir and the Zed Xsani. To grasp the vault's secrets for herself, Sakamir had become the arch traitor and accepted the tattoo of a Zed. To Constants, this was the worst crime imaginable. Xsani's fervent thirst for power had persuaded her to accept an alliance with an Alban turncoat – behaviour that went clean against everything she had ever been told. Both women knew their union was based purely on convenience.

Mistrust between them crackled like kindling.

Xsani had never seen a book. She knew about writing and words – she had gazed on faded remnants of Long Dead language – but she had no idea how to decipher them. Sakamir guessed this and relished the power it gave her. Her first plan was to explain the alphabet incorrectly so her rival would be unable to read if she ever got her hands on a book. But thinking this through, she realised that to keep up the pretence she'd have to invent a whole language. In the end, she opted to teach Xsani what she had learned from Cyrus. After all, she told herself, the lisping vixen would be dead before she had an opportunity to use any new skills she acquired.

The lessons, conducted each morning in a corner of the piazza, were not a success. Xsani was impatient and Sakamir, with only a few days' reading experience, was unsure of her subject. Matters came to a head on the fifth day when Xsani brought out four words copied from the wall inside her headquarters and asked Sakamir to read them.

"You mistrust me?" retorted Sakamir.

"Of courthe not. I am jutht interethted, thath all. Pleath tell me what it thayth."

"Right. As I have told you, that shape is an H and this one is an E and this one an R followed by another E. Together they make a word."

"What word?"

"It's pronounced 'hairy', I think."

"And the next word?"

"Well, it begins with an L, followed by I, E and S. That's

pronounced 'liaise'.

"Go on. Pleathe."

By the time Sakamir had interpreted 'Here lies Mary Clough' as 'Hairy liaise marry clog', the Malika had had enough. No more reading lessons, she announced. She would wait until they were in possession of the Soterion. Then she would force that literate Constant – what was his name? Ah yes, Cyrus – she would force Cyrus or one of his pupils to teach her. In fact, she mused to Jinsha later that evening, she was looking forward to meeting this Cyrus. From what Sakamir said, he sounded quite interesting for a dumbman. The Kogon must ensure he was not killed when they took over Alba.

Giv's education, in contrast to the Malika's, went exceptionally well. His teacher was a Constant woman of sixteen winters whom the Kogon had captured while raiding for breeding slaves. Finding the prisoner could count, reason and speak fluently, Xsani had agreed to spare her life if she bred and, while feeding her baby, passed on her skills to the Zektivs. Presented with little alternative, the woman agreed.

As with all captured Constants, the woman was given no name. She was referred to simply as 'Teach'. To begin with, she was terrified of Giv. In her mind, a man with a Z tattoo meant only one thing. Rape. Although she never completely overcame her fear, she soon saw that Giv was fairly harmless. In fact, he was almost as frightened as she was. Before his lessons began, he was given a close inspection of the Malika's bodyguard and told that if he laid a finger on Teach or any of the Kogon, he would suffer the same fate as the guards and then die. Slowly.

Timur had taught Giv to count to five, the number of his fingers on one hand. Guided by a less brutal instructor, he mastered the rest of his numbers in a few days. He picked up the skill of speaking in sentences and new vocabulary soaked into his brain like rain into desert sand. Gazing at him with sad, red-rimmed eyes, Teach wondered what this young man would have been like had he not been born a Zed.

One afternoon, after he had been at his lessons for barely half a moon, Giv sensed someone standing behind him as he worked out how to add seven to five.

"Giv – er, I – know the answer," he said, eager to show off his new speech to the unseen spectator. "Seven and five is – wait – yes, twelve!"

"Exthelent, Giv!"

His heart leaped. She was here, his Malika, the one he adored as much as the great Timur! He turned to look up at her, grinning madly.

"You – think I – am – making – progrush, my Mighty Malika?" he spluttered.

"Progreth, yeth. You will thoon be ready to go to work."

"Anything you say is the joy of Giv," he responded inanely.

Xsani raised a quizzical eyebrow. "Really? We thall thpeak again in five dayth' time."

Giv's task was straightforward – though hardly simple. Sakamir insisted that the capture of the Soterion, which she called 'Operation Alba', needed more warriors. Xsani was not so sure, but in the end she accepted her ally's advice and gave Giv the task of winning over at least one other tribe of Zeds. He had little experience of leadership and none of negotiation. What he did have was a quick mind and a passionate devotion to both the Malika of the Kogon and the head of Timur, his dead Malik.

To inspire him further, Xsani actually touched him as he was leaving. Briefly taking his hand in hers, she told him he was her favourite dumbman. Since she hated the whole species, this was hardly a compliment. But Giv was not to know this and in his memory the moment lay like an eternal jewel, more precious than life itself. Later that day, to Sakamir's astonishment, she actually caught him skipping rather than walking when he thought no one was looking.

The key to Giv's mission was Timur's head. Were he to approach a Zed tribe without it, he would be slaughtered before he opened his mouth. Xsani and Sakamir knew his, but their frail coalition was strained almost to breaking point when they discussed how the precious totem might be used. Sakamir wanted to accompany Giv herself and act as guardian of the head. Xsani would have none of it. Eventually, they agreed on a party of twelve. Giv, the official head-bearer, would travel with five Grozny, handpicked for their relative competence. To balance them, Jinsha and Yalisha would lead a party of six Kogon.

For some time, Xsani's scouts had been scouring the region in search of a suitable Zed tribe with whom to ally. The first group they came across, the Flid, were so low on numbers that they faced extinction within a year or so. An alliance with them would be pointless. The second tribe, the four-hundred-strong Dangalon, were the complete opposite. Their Malik, the famously unreliable Sintz, would turn on his allies whenever it suited him. No, Sakamir and Xsani agreed, they wouldn't risk approaching the Dangalon.

The Gurkov, on the other hand, were an altogether different prospect. They were a reasonably large group – about the same size as the Grozny – and like them they had a reputation for discipline and tough fighting. These qualities owed much to the leadership of their commander, Malik Ogg. From a distance Ogg's short trunk, from which thick, hairy arms and legs sprouted like branches, gave the impression of a walking tree. His mind was similarly wooden in a no-nonsense way. In his yes–no world, there were only ever two alternatives: good–bad; Zed–Constant; male–female – he couldn't conceive of anything in between.

Xsani's scouts found one aspect of Ogg's character intensely distasteful – his addiction to breeding. Every day, they reported, he tried at least once to increase the size of his tribe. Xsani and Sakamir were not impressed. Nevertheless, in their eyes the lustful Malik had one overwhelming point in his favour. He had heard of the Grozny and regarded Malik Timur as the ultimate Zed leader. Moreover, he did not appear to have heard that his hero was dead.

On the evening before their departure, Giv's Kogon and Grozny escorts were brought together for the first time. Although they had been prepared for this, both groups were clearly uneasy, shuffling their feet and glancing warily at each other. Xsani and Sakamir, hoping the power of the head would prove greater than traditional hatred, had arranged a small ceremony of unity before the dark totem.

Speaking through Xsani, Timur reminded the mission of their loyalty to him and his cause. He was planning to return to Alba in triumph as commander of a great army of Zeds. Their task was to assemble that army. Nothing – particularly inter-Zed rivalry – must get in their way. The ceremony concluded with the rousing slogan: "Under mighty Over-Malik, all Zeds are one!"

"Under mighty Over-Malik, all Zeds are one!" chorused the chosen twelve until Xsani signalled them to stop. Even while chanting of unity, she noticed, the Grozny and Kogon had tried to out-do each other. Mixing Zed men and women would always be dangerous, but there was no other way of assembling a force powerful enough to seize Alba and its precious Soterion. For a prize of such magnitude, any risk was worth taking.

Soon after sunrise, Timur's head was wrapped in dried grass and placed in a wooden box strapped to Giv's back. Xsani and Sakamir bade the embassy farewell and watched in silence as it set out for the region where the Gurkov had last been spotted.

While the Grozny and Kogon were within the forest, all went according to plan. The trouble began when they left the trees and entered a broad and scrubby plain. The wider horizons seemed to free the Zeds' minds of the limitations imposed upon them and they quickly reverted to type. Giv had done his best to prevent this happening. After the Timur ceremony the previous evening, he had reinforced its message by speaking severely to his men. Jinsha, Yalisha and the other Kogon were not like other flabtoads, he explained. They were not playmates. Had the Grozny forgotten what was done to Gawlip when he tried to amuse himself with a milking flabtoad? Grand Malik Jamshid had ordered him to be whipped and a flaming brand applied to his left hand. The flesh had burned away so completely that he was now known as Bonefingers. That would be the punishment, Giv decreed, if any of them so much as touched a Kogon.

But strong words were not enough.

Under Timur's harsh tuition, Giv had the makings of an effective Zed commander. But his infatuation with Xsani and his lessons with Teach had softened him. He was confused by the change. He still used the merciless language of a Grozny, but he found it increasingly incomplete and strangely unsatisfying. Like an explorer stumbling across a land of unexpected loveliness, he had discovered a part of his mind he had not previously been aware of, a region where colours were subtler, vistas broader, sounds more harmonious. Words like 'beauty', which had previously been meaningless or even offensive, were beginning to make sense.

The Grozny sensed the change in their Captain, though they could not put it into words. They respected him as the man who had brought back Malik Timur, but they were not afraid of him. And a Grozny leader who could not terrify was always going to struggle.

Jinsha noticed the problem first. She was walking beside Giv at the rear of the column. Yalisha was out in front, flanked by two Kogon. The five Grozny warriors followed a short distance behind her while the two remaining Kogon spread out on either side to prevent ambush.

"Those dumbmans are trouble," said Jinsha, pointing at the Grozny ambling along in front of them.

Giv looked up to see one of his men making obscene gestures behind Yalisha's back. His colleagues roared with laughter and repeated the gestures with gusto.

"Volebrains, do you want to be bonefingers?" shouted Giv. The Grozny nudged each other and stopped their horseplay for a while. When it restarted, shortly before midday, it took an altogether uglier form. The Zed on the right of the column, unable to control himself any longer, made a sudden lunge at the Kogon ahead of him, pulled her to the ground and began clawing at her leather clothing.

Yalisha, hearing the woman's shouts of protest, spun round and thrust her lance into the man's neck, killing him instantly. The column swiftly disintegrated into a vicious melee of stabbing and hacking. A blow from a heavy iron club smashed open the head of the first woman to be attacked, and the stomach of another on Yalisha's left was torn by a swinging gut-ripper. Moments later, three Grozny were bleeding heavily from deep wounds inflicted by Kogon spears.

To the astonishment of everyone, not least himself, Giv's prompt action saved the embassy from annihilation. He fell into a sort of trance immediately the fight broke out. He undid the rope that held the wooden box on his back, lowered it to the ground, lifted out the blackened totem and raised it above his head. When he spoke – he had no idea how – it was not with his own voice but with Timur's. The effect was mesmerising.

"Ratpizzles!" he screamed in the high-pitched tones familiar to every Grozny. "What is this dunghead behaviour? Throw down your weapons, weasel-scum, before I peel off your skin for shoes!"

The fight stopped at once. The astonished combatants lowered their weapons to the sandy ground and looked sheepishly around at the damage they had caused. Two of the Kogon warriors were already dead and a third was dying of her wounds. As only one Grozny had been killed outright, it looked as if the men had come off better. But three of them were losing so much blood they couldn't continue. Jinsha ordered them to leave at once. Giv gave his consent and the men limped off unsteadily towards the forest. All three died before they reached the shelter of the trees.

The embassy had shrunk to five: three Kogon and two Grozny. Nonetheless, what it had lost in size, it had gained in unity. Even Jinsha and Yalisha respected Giv: walking in their midst was a dumbman so clever he could assume the form of one who had died. He was not just guardian of the head – he was guardian of its spirit, too. Inside Captain Giv, Timur the Terrible lived on.

Back in Alba, Sammy's suggestion that Cyrus could cure Jalus had tested his friend's patience to the limit. "What on earth did you say that for?" he fumed when they were alone in the empty Ghasar. "Your big mouth has wrecked the whole mission!" His face contorted with waves of anger and frustration.

Sammy was genuinely taken aback. "What you talking

about, Cyrus?" he protested, forgetting the correct grammar he had learned recently. "Course you can cure him! You cured me, easy as shooting rabbits – and I had a great hole in my leg. All that's wrong with Jalus is a bit of the shivers."

"Bit of the shivers?" cried Cyrus. "You just don't get it, do you?"

"Course I do! If I hadn't come up with my plan, Bahm would've put a stop to everything. Then where'd we be?"

"Same as we are now."

"Come on, Cyrus! Don't be so hard on me. You've got a chance to put a stop to Bahm's nonsense once and for all."

"It's Yash, too. And you've given them an even better chance of ending our mission, Sammy."

"So it's up to you to make sure you win out." Sammy's face softened. "I meaned it, Cyrus, I really did. I've seen everything you've done – well, almost all of it – and I reckon there's nothing you can't do if you sets your mind to it. Nothing."

Cyrus rubbed his hands over his face. "I don't have much choice, do I? Cure Jalus or say goodbye to the Soterion." Sammy nodded. "Right, I'd better go and see if there's something I can do to help the lad. I doubt it, though."

"You might doubt it," Sammy grinned, "but I don't!"

"Fool!" muttered Cyrus, giving the young man a friendly slap on the shoulder. "Come on! Let's go and find Jalus."

Even before he entered the room in which Jalus lay, Cyrus knew from the smell what was wrong with the boy. Diarrhoea. The vile, dehydrating illness was the scourge of both Constant and

Zed alike. It swept through settlements and tribes, disabling adults and killing scores of children. Because it was known to be highly infectious, Alban victims of more than two winters were immediately isolated in the Alone, a small wooden hut high among the terraces above the Soterion Gate. Sufferers were left with drinking water, a foul-smelling toilet bucket and hay with which to clean themselves. Twice a day, an archer carried the bucket away to be emptied and replenished the water. The chances of recovery were slight.

Telling Sammy and Corby to remain outside, Cyrus took a deep breath and opened the door of the Alone. A glance around the room told him all he needed. His heart sank. Jalus, naked and covered in sweat, lay on a low bed with a curtain of long black hair plastered across his yellow brow and cheek. His eyelids barely flicked when Cyrus gently stroked his head and whispered his name. One day at the most, Cyrus thought. Glancing at the toilet bucket on the way out, he noticed flecks of blood floating on the surface. He groaned inwardly. No, not even a day. The boy was doomed.

"Well?" asked Sammy as Cyrus emerged into the fresh air. "How can we make him better?"

"We can't. He'll probably be dead by nightfall."

Sammy shook his head. "Without us even trying? He wouldn't die if the Long Dead was here to look after him. Come on! You can find out what they'd do, can't you? It'll be in that Aid book."

Where does this fellow's optimism come from? Cyrus wondered. Looking into Sammy's open face, he knew he couldn't let him down. However grim the chances, he had to try.

As quickly and carefully as possible, he explained to Sammy what he had learned of contamination and the importance of cleanliness. He instructed him to carry Jalus out of the stinking hut, lie him in the shade, wash him thoroughly all over and persuade him to drink as much as possible. It might be a good idea to keep Corby away from him, too. Meanwhile, he would run back to the Soterion and see if there was anything in *First Aid and Basic Medicine* that might help.

To his surprise, on the way down the terraces, Cyrus met Miouda coming in the opposite direction. She knew how desperate the situation was and wondered if she could help.

"Thanks, Miouda. Thanks so much!" Cyrus panted. "Just go up there and boil water! Anyhow, anywhere – and as much as you can get hold of." Miouda nodded and turned to continue up the slope.

"No, wait! Throw away what's left in the water jug. It's filthy! Then get Jalus to drink as much of the water you've boiled as you can. Wash him in it, too."

"Right. But where're you off to, Cyrus? Aren't you needed up there?" She pointed to the hut.

"It'll be alright now you're here. I need to get down to the Ghasar and see what that first aid book says about Jalus' illness."

With an affectionate squeeze of his friend's hand, Cyrus was off down the slope again, calling over his shoulder, "And while you're about it, wash Sammy as well! He's bound to have got muck all over him!"

The terraces were deep in shadow by the time he had

finished searching out references to diarrhoea in his first aid book. Struggling with the technical vocabulary and cursing when most of the treatments suggested medicines he couldn't possibly get hold of, he finally worked out a strategy. Hurrying out of the Ghasar, he grabbed an armful of fruits from the nearest storeroom and set out for the Alone.

He was astonished at the transformation his friends had brought about. Jalus lay on a bed of fresh straw beside the hut. His physical appearance had changed little, though he was cleaner and the hair had been combed off his forehead. Miouda knelt at his side, alternately wiping his brow with a damp cloth and trying to get him to take sips of water from the cup she held to his lips. Bowls of boiled water were arranged on a low terrace wall nearby. A little further off, Sammy and other members of Cyrus' Soterion class were tending a blazing fire over which water bubbled in an iron pot. Corby, upright and alert, sat on the terrace above and surveyed the whole scene like a sentry.

Miouda looked up as Cyrus approached. No change, she mouthed. He turned to give instructions to the small group of helpers. Jalus was dying of dehydration. Somehow they had to get liquid, clean liquid, inside him. Fruit juice was best, together with water. Leaving Sammy and his helpers to squeeze juice into bowls washed with boiled water, he began scouring the terraces. When he had found a suitable hollow reed, he gave Sammy his instructions, rinsed his hands in boiled water and knelt beside Jalus on the opposite side to Miouda.

The sick boy's tongue was black and swollen, making it impossible for him to swallow. After Miouda had raised his head so he wouldn't choke, Cyrus carefully pushed the boy's tongue to one side and inserted the reed into his mouth. He made a funnel with his hands and held it over the top of the reed. When all was ready, Sammy poured a mixture of juice and water into Cyrus' cupped hands.

At first nothing happened. Then, very slowly, the mixture drained down the straw. Jalus coughed and Miouda adjusted the reed so the liquid went down his throat and not into his windpipe.

The treatment continued throughout the night. Although Jalus had to be carried over to the bucket twice more before dawn, his fever subsided and by first light he was sleeping soundly. Shortly afterwards, having heard what was going on, Yash and Bahm climbed up to the Alone and stood watching in silence.

By nightfall on the second day, Jalus was out of danger. He slept most of the time. When he awoke, he was able to speak and drink unassisted. The treatment of the Long Dead had worked.

As the patient was finally being carried back to the settlement, Cyrus walked wearily over to Sammy and Miouda. "We did it!" he gasped, throwing his arms round them and holding them close. With tears in his eyes, he thanked them with all his heart.

"We've saved the Soterion!" grinned Miouda, holding on to Cyrus as tightly as he held her.

"Not just us," said Sammy. "The Long Dead. We couldn't have done it without them, could we?"

Cyrus laughed. "Of course not. And they've proved to us, to everyone, why we must go on and on until we have made a brave new world out of the ruins of the old one." Letting go of his companions, he turned to the fire. "And as a sign, watch!"

He strode over to the fire, pulled out a blazing branch and held it to the wall of the Alone. Soon the filthy wooden hut was burning fiercely.

"There!" he cried as he watched the flames rise into the night sky. "An end to dirt and ignorance!"

Malik Ogg opened one eye and grunted. Something was not right. The sky was clear, the stars were bright, around him the Gurkov lay sleeping... But all was not well. There was an unusual noise. He propped himself up on one elbow and listened. From his left came the whimpering of a breeding slave. He couldn't have been woken by such routine snivelling, he told himself. Must be something else. Ah! What was that? There was another sound, a new and different one. It wasn't the wind and it wasn't an animal...

Ogg rose, grasped his sword firmly in his right hand, and sniffed. There was no unusual scent to give him a clue. Still the noise went on. A sort of moaning whisper, it came from the trees directly in front of him. Cautiously, he moved closer and stood listening to the beckoning tones floating out of the darkness. "Maliko!" they seemed to say. "Maliko."

As he peered into the gloom, a flickering light appeared. He gripped his sword tighter and advanced a couple of steps. All of a sudden, he realised what the sound was. Someone was calling his name. "Malik Ogg," it chanted in a strange, high-pitched voice. "Malik Ogg."

"Yes?" he answered, keeping his voice low so as not to wake any of his tribesmen. Whatever was going on, it was for him alone and he didn't want any stone-headed Gurkov blundering in on it.

"Advance and look on me!"

Ogg did as he was told. He was a straightforward, blunt man without a smidgeon of imagination in all his Z-stamped body. Nevertheless, he was intrigued. The light, a crude candle that Jinsha had brought with her, was something he had never seen before. Of much greater interest was what hung above it: a blackened head suspended by its hair from an overhanging branch. In the flickering darkness, it looked as if the head itself was speaking.

"Listen carefully, Malik Ogg," the voice continued. "I am Over-Malik Timur the Terrible. I bring you great news. The time of the Zeds has come. We are gathering together to make a great army. We will crush the Constants and all their riches and knowledge will be ours. Soon Zeds will rule the world."

Ogg scratched his head. He was no fool, but all this ruling the world business stretched his understanding to its limits – and beyond. "And Ogg," he muttered, "what does Ogg do?"

"Join our army, great Ogg. Three in one: I will bring together the Zeds of Grozny, Gurkov and Kogon."

Ogg stared suspiciously at the shimmering head. He'd never heard of the Kogon – who were they? "Maybe," he responded. "And if I don't?"

"If you do not join, Ogg, the fury of Timur will fall upon you. His revenge will be terrible."

Ogg gave an uncertain snort.

"But if you join with me," the head continued in more flattering tones, "I will reward you. Ogg will have his desire."

"Desire?" echoed the Malik as he struggled to come to terms with the head's sudden shift of mood.

"Timur knows your wishes, Ogg. The Over-Malik understands your deep desires. This is what you want, isn't it?" As the voice was speaking, two female forms slipped seductively into the candlelight, one on either side of the head. Both were naked.

Ogg gasped and took a step forward.

"Wait!" commanded the voice. "Feast your eyes! If you follow me, these slaves are yours – they and as many others as there are trees in the forest. All as soft as doe skin and as smooth as milk! Look on them, Ogg! Dream on them! Tomorrow my man Giv will come to you and explain all. These slaves will then be for you, just you. Tomorrow and tomorrow and tomorrow …"

As the voice faded, the candle blew out and the bewildered Malik heard a rustling in the dark ahead of him. When he went to investigate, the totem had gone.

But the images in his head burned on. Timur, the mightiest Zed of all, had spoken to him. What an honour to fight with him! Together the Grozny and the Gurkov would be unstoppable!

Ogg stumbled back to his sleeping place, lay down and closed his eyes. Timur and succulent slave bodies – it was almost more than he could manage. "Oh come, tomorrow!" he panted. "Come! Come! Come!"

7

In the Dark

Sleep, which normally fell upon Jamshid like a hammer, did not come easily. What go wrong? he asked himself again and again. Timur tell Jamshid attack; Jamshid attack; Jamshid's men die. Why?

The question nagged away in the Grand Malik's ponderous brain all the way back to Filna. As he entered the forest that cloaked the ruined town, he stopped and leaned heavily against a tree. What sort of reception awaited him? The old Timur rewarded failure with harsh punishment. How would the new Timur, the Over-Malik, react? He had ordered Jamshid to lead an assault on Alba, hadn't he? And the mysterious Malika had agreed, saying Jamshid's role was very important.

He lifted his fur cap and scratched angrily at his lice-ridden scalp. Something was not right. He didn't know what it was, but he was starting to wonder whether it might involve Malika Xsani. She couldn't possibly be deceiving Timur, could she?

There was only one way to find out. With a final rub of his head, Jamshid replaced his hat and set off again into the forest.

Immediately the Eyes spotted him, they informed Xsani, who ordered him to be brought to her before he made contact with his fellow Grozny.

"Tho you have returned," she began when the burly Zed was kneeling before her on the balcony. "Alone, I thee. What happened?"

Jamshid explained, to the best of his limited ability, how he had obeyed Timur's orders and attacked Alba. Xsani raised a quizzical eyebrow when she heard how his force had marched out into open ground and been shot down like sheep. In future operations, she decided, the Grozny would have no task involving either strategy or skill.

"And how did Jamthid ethcape?" she asked.

The Grand Malik twisted his hands anxiously, expecting a blow or stab. He ran away, he confessed – but only so he could fight again.

"You *ran away*?" With a wave of the hand, Xsani ordered her bodyguard to come over and stand in a silent circle round him. For a while the quiet of the afternoon was broken only by birdsong and the sound of urine trickling down Jamshid's legs, soaking into the hem of his fur coat and gathering in a pool about his knees. The Malika wrinkled her nose in disgust.

"Are you afraid of me, Malik?"

"Not understand!" he blurted. "I obey Timur orders. He tell Jamshid –"

"Ah! Tho it ith the Over-Malik you are afraid of, yeth?"

"Yes!" he gasped, before denying it with equal force. "No!" As he raised his eyes to hers, his great, ugly, scarred face twitched like a sleeping dog. "Jamshid lost!" he wailed, almost pitifully. "Not understand nothing!"

Seeing he was out of his depth emotionally and intellectually, Xsani had a decision to make. Dispense with him or keep him to control the Grozny? She opted for the latter, binding him tighter to her with what she hoped would be a powerful pact. They would not tell Timur about his failure – his running away would be their own little secret.

The speed of Giv's development surprised everyone, including himself. His skill in mimicking the sound of Timur's voice was matched by an extraordinary ability to use his hero's vocabulary. Moreover, he continued to believe the Over-Malik was speaking through him, that his words really were Timur's and that he, the humble Captain Giv, was merely a mouthpiece. This gave his pronouncements real authenticity. Noticing this early on, Jinsha had used it when planning the recruitment of Malik Ogg. She knew of Ogg's obsession with women, and added the temptation of naked women to honey the trap. She did not see the danger of making Ogg a promise they had no intention of keeping.

Giv kept up his performance the next morning when he marched boldly into the Gurkov camp as an emissary from Over-Malik Timur. Ogg, still burning with memories of the previous night, received him at once and agreed to join the Grozny–Kogon coalition under Timur's generalship. An assault on a Constant community was just the sort of thing he enjoyed. He wasn't entirely sure what the Soterion was – nor was Giv – but the idea of defying the Death Month was certainly appealing.

Throughout the discussions, Giv trod carefully around the subject of Xsani. He mentioned her name, calling her Timur's 'officer'. But knowing Ogg needed educating in the new ways, as he himself had been, he avoided the word 'Malika' and reference to the gender of the Kogon and their leader. This was just as well. As the negotiations were drawing to a close Ogg asked about the slaves he had been promised. Feigning ignorance, Giv asked what he meant.

"In the night," drooled Ogg, "Timur showed me two slaves with thighs like gold and –"

"Ah!" interrupted Giv. "Yes, mighty Timur has a whole tribe of slaves like that, all unused and all for Ogg."

The Malik grinned and rubbed himself in a primitive fashion. "Where are they?"

"Waiting with Mali – er, with Officer Xsani. The sooner we get there, the sooner they will be yours, great Ogg."

The promise of giving Ogg female slaves annoyed Jinsha and Yalisha; but since the original idea had been theirs, they went along with it. They were delighted with the rest of Giv's bargaining. Like Teach, they wondered how different he might be had he not been born a Grozny.

The journey back to Filna passed without incident. On arrival, the Gurkov were settled some distance from the town and from the Grozny. Ogg stayed with his men until nightfall when Giv, guided by the calls of the Eyes, led him to the smoke-filled sty. After the leaves had had their effect, he was introduced to the Timur totem in much the same way as Giv and Jamshid. The ceremony differed only in three small but important details. Xsani, Sakamir and the two Zektivs masked their faces and wore shapeless clothing, the word 'Malika' was omitted and, on Jinsha's recommendation, Giv spoke the words of the totem. The show left Ogg wedded to the coalition, besotted with the Over-Malik and in awe of his mysterious officer, Xsani.

Nevertheless, he was a man of very basic instincts. A fuzzy head, mysterious rituals and moonlight were all very well, but they were only part of the reason why he had brought the Gurkov to the coalition. The vision of the naked slaves still haunted him. Timur had promised them to him and he wanted them. Right now. So, when after two days' camp near Filna they still had not appeared, he grew restless. Someone was thwarting the will of the Over-Malik, he decided. But who? The obvious people to ask were his new allies, the Grozny.

The fire in the Alone brought Yash hurrying up the terraces to see what was going on. When Sammy explained to him, he glared angrily at the blaze for a while before confronting Cyrus. "Suppose you think you can do that sort of thing now, eh?"

Cyrus was too exhausted to take in what he meant. "Sorry, Yash – what sort of thing?"

"Setting fire to Alban property without my permission."

"Oh that! The hut was doing more harm than good – and with luck it won't be needed any more."

Yash snorted in frustration. "Listen, Cyrus. You tricked your way out of trouble that time, didn't you? I'm not stupid, you know: you got Sammy to set up that little test which you knew you'd pass. And it's made you a bit of a hero. Clap, clap!"

His eyes narrowed and, staring straight at Cyrus, he continued, "But I warn you, it's the last time you make a fool of me. Got it?"

"Come on Yash, you've got it all wrong," began Cyrus. "Sammy and I didn't set up anything –"

"And you expect me to believe that? Huh! Just watch it, ok? Next time my authority's challenged I won't be so understanding." So saying, he turned and strode off into the darkness.

Cyrus shrugged and joined Sammy and Miouda as they returned to the settlement. Before going to his dormitory, he called in at the Ghasar to think over what had happened. The building's interior was dark and still. Groping his way over to his customary chair, he sat wearily down and let the evocative smell of books wash around him. It reminded him of the moment he had opened the Soterion door and for the first time encountered the magical aroma of leather, ink, glue and paper. He thought of it as the 'scent of learning'. Sometimes he was content simply to bury his nose in a book rather than read it. He wondered whether the Long Dead had ever done the same. Perhaps, because books were so common then, they had simply taken them for granted?

His mind turned to Jalus and the information in *First Aid and Basic Medicine*. Wasn't it strange how black marks on a white page – 'squiggles' Yash had dismissed them as – had saved a child's life? How clever it was to think of making words into shapes so others, at different times and in different places, could understand them! How many people's ideas and dreams and reasonings were stored in the volumes stacked around him? It was beyond his conception. And Yash had talked so casually of carting them all back into the vault.

Cyrus lay back in his chair, yawned and closed his eyes. Why couldn't the Emir see what a tragic waste it would be to lock the books up again? He had no imagination, that was his problem. He was also a fool. When the books were returned to the vault, only the person with the key would be able to get at them… And that, of course, was Yash…

In his dream, Yash and Timur were coming out of the Ghasar with armfuls of books. Cyrus was down the well in Lion Square, shouting at them to stop what they were doing. "Leave them!" he cried, his words echoing round the shaft without ever reaching the top. Bahm's laughing face blotted out the sky above and he threw down a round and heavy object that struck Cyrus on the shoulder. He looked into the water where it had fallen to see Timur's face staring up at him. Now he was climbing out. In the thronging square, mocking Zeds had replaced the Albans, and Roxanne and Miouda were being paraded before him, both cruelly bound in chains.

He was running through crowds of Zeds who chanted something incomprehensible about Timur's head. They clawed at him as he fought his way along the path in a desperate effort to reach the Soterion. Yash and Sakamir, with oversized and bloody Z tattoos branded into their foreheads, were guarding the steel door. "It's ours!" they taunted. "All ours!" He tried to get at them, but the Zeds pulled him back, tearing his clothes with nails like talons.

"It's not yours!" he shouted. "Not yours! Not yours!"

He woke with a start in the darkened Ghasar. It was only a dream, thank goodness, a fantasy like in *The Odyssey* where men were turned into pigs. Things like that just don't happen, he told himself. Sakamir and Yash were Constants – they had been raised as Constants and thought like Constants. It would be inconceivable for such people to have anything to do with Zed barbarians…

Curling up in his chair, he decided not to return to the dormitory but to spend the night where he was. The place inspired him, gave him strength to continue. He had already shown how the knowledge of the Long Dead could improve the daily lives of all Constants. It was his duty to carry on.

An opportunity came the next day, when one of the four Konnels responsible for Alban children under the age of eight approached him and asked whether the cure that had worked on Jalus would work on others. Of course, he replied – and before long he found himself instructing those who ran the nursery in the basic principles of avoiding and treating diarrhoea. In the afternoon, he began going through first aid with his students. The idea was to make them capable of doing what he had done with Sammy and Miouda. The entire class would become healers of the sick.

Cyrus had a new status, too. When he first arrived in

Alba, he was seen as an exotic Outsider, a good-looking and brave man who had helped Roxanne open the Soterion. This position was then undermined by Yash's hostility and Bahm's criticisms. The burly conservative blamed Cyrus for upsetting the regular pattern of their lives, and scorned the quest for the Salvation Project because it threatened to replace the quick, clean and certain Death Month with a protracted, slow and uncertain end.

The Jalus incident had not just restored Cyrus' prestige, it had increased it considerably. The entire community was moved by the recovery of a child whom they had believed to be dying. Slowly, as more people were healed of their illnesses and injuries, death came to be seen as something to be fought against. And Cyrus, the inspiration behind the reform, was hailed as a hero. He was almost what the Long Dead would have called a prophet. His judgement was asked on all kinds of matters, such as whether he thought so-and-so would make a good copemate. The five boys born since his arrival were all named Cyrus.

Bahm, always straightforward and honest, went along with the new thinking. "I still don't like the idea of living on and on until I'm a rotting bag of loony bones," he confessed when Sammy had told him what life was like before the Great Death. "But I suppose a fair bit of that Soterion stuff is pretty useful." He had a special interest in firing pottery in a charcoal kiln.

Only Yash resisted the general trend. The more praise was heaped on Cyrus, the less civil the Emir was towards him. As the days passed, he became increasingly tetchy about Sakamir's absence, too. Even his military skills, previously second to none, began to falter. He reduced the number of lookouts on the walls and turned down requests for patrols. "We're quite safe enough," he retorted on one occasion, "unless Cyrus goes bringing in some Z-marked woman again." He tried to cover the insensitive remark with a laugh, but no one was taken in. Roxanne's star had risen alongside Cyrus': to mock someone who had sacrificed her life for the Constant cause was in very poor taste.

"He's just plain jealous of you," Bahm declared one day. "And I don't like it."

"Maybe," replied Cyrus. "But I can understand how he feels. To be honest, his decision-making's a greater worry."

"Aye," Bahm agreed. "You know, only yesterday I was certain I'd seen summat moving out beyond the Patrol Gate. It weren't a wolf and it weren't so small as a rabbit. Hiding in the trees, it was. Watching. It were a Zed, as sure as my name's Bahm – but the Emir said no patrol was going out, so that was it."

"Yes, it's infuriating. But we've got to be so careful, Bahm. Yash was chosen by the people. If we undermine that principle, everything falls apart."

Bahm frowned. "Suppose so. But it makes me very uncomfortable, Cyrus."

Me too, thought Cyrus. It was almost as if Yash was weakening Alba's defences deliberately. But that was impossible, wasn't it? Things like that happened only in nightmares.

Cyrus spent his mornings working on ways to improve Alban life, and his afternoons reading and teaching. He had never been so busy. With Bahm and Sammy he was experimenting with metal smelting, building a water mill to grind corn, and setting up two furnaces for firing pottery. Other members of his class, headed by the fifteen- and sixteen-year-old 'seniors', learned about candles and lamps lit by vegetable oils. Their first attempts resulted in more burned fingers than light. In time, when they had mastered how to make a wick, they provided all the sleeping quarters with an emergency night light. Miouda's personal triumph – a sundial that stood beside the well – came from her study of how the Long Dead divided a day into hours and minutes. She also explained the term 'Death Month' by discovering that 'month' was the Long Dead term for what the Constants knew as a 'moon'.

The afternoon school was no longer a matter of Cyrus standing and dictating. His role had developed into that of principal teacher among several. Four more young Albans had joined Jalus, Poso and the other beginners. Two seniors took it in turns to instruct them in reading and writing. Miouda and the fourth senior worked with the middle group. All the older students, including Sammy and Yash, studied on their own. At the end of the day, they met together to share ideas and discuss what they had learned.

An individual was invited to lead the daily discussion – 'seminar', Cyrus called it. With Yash the talk was nearly always about the Salvation Project or the Long Dead's weapons. What fools their ancestors were to have destroyed all firearms as they were dying out, he declared. He had read of a device called a 'machine gun' and dreamed of positioning one on the walls of Alba. The only other subject he raised was a drink he had researched called 'wine'. He wasn't yet sure of the details, but the Long Dead seemed to have great fun with it. When he had time, he announced, he'd do further research.

Cyrus urged him to be careful. "I've read about this wine stuff, too," he explained. "It changed people's minds. Made them happy, yes, but also made them sad – and violent sometimes. Probably best to leave it for the moment, Yash."

"Thank you for your wise advice, Mister Scholar," drawled the Emir in a voice that dripped with sarcasm. "But with your permission, I'll decide for myself what I do."

Cyrus exchanged glances with Miouda but said nothing.

Sammy's topic was based on his upbringing with the Children of Gova. Their settlement was protected by a very powerful electric fence. Roxanne, who had come across electricity in the IKEA catalogue, one of the three books she had read, was the first to understand the force behind the fence. But she had not seen the relationship between the electric current and the settlement's huge solar panels. It needed Sammy's patient research to figure this out.

"Now, this is how I see it," he told the seminar on one occasion. "This stuff 'electricity' is a sort of power made of 'particles'. I looked that word up but it didn't help, so let's forget it.

"Anyway, electricity goes through metal wires like water through a pipe. It runs along really, really quick. And you can't see it, which makes it pretty weird stuff. When it gets to the end, it can stop or do something."

"Eh? 'Do something' – what's that mean?" asked the man on

Miouda's right.

Sammy thought for a moment. "Well, it's a sort of force, right? Like the wind. The Long Dead got it doing loads of things, like powering lights and making cars go."

"Cars?"

"Sorry. You've not been far out of Alba so you've never seen one of them rusty things with wheels, have you?" The young man shook his head. "Cars is what the Long Dead travelled in. I'll show you a picture of one after this."

"Thanks."

Sammy resumed his presentation. "What I'm really interested in is making electricity. They did it in the Gova place I come from with a whopping great panel. Black, it was, and made of a sort of glass.

"On our way here," he went on, waving his hands about in excitement, "we saw smaller panels like that on the roofs of Long Dead houses. They were mostly all covered by ivy and other stuff, but if we went out and got one, and brought it back here, I reckon –"

"No!" It was Yash. Standing up and pointing at Sammy, he went on angrily, "Don't you understand? I'm the Emir of Alba and I decide whether a patrol goes out or not. You and Cyrus come in here and think you can take over the place. Well, you can't!"

With that, he left the building and the seminar came to an early close.

After the others had gone, Cyrus and Miouda were left alone with their books. They often sat like this, quietly reading together until it was too dark to continue. Their friendship was deeper, more relaxed since the evening, several days previous, when they had drawn back the invisible curtain hanging between them.

"Miouda?"

"Yes?"

"It's about Roxanne…"

"I wondered when you'd mention it, Cyrus." She paused. "I know she was exceptional, a remarkable person in every way. And I'm not like her. I couldn't be even if I tried – and I'm not sure I'd want to be. Everyone's different. But I'm not a child and I'm not jealous." She smiled. "And it doesn't stop me liking you."

"Nor me you, Miouda. A lot. And I'm so glad you understand. But you have someone…"

"Had."

"Ah! I hoped so."

Miouda made rapid progress in her literacy and they had got into the habit of reading the same book, one after the other, then talking about it. Frequently it was not the stories or the information they discussed, but the meaning of individual words. So many were alien to them because the concepts they represented had been lost.

In the years immediately after the Great Death, while the Constant settlements were fighting off Zed attacks almost daily, there was no place for weakness or sentimentality. Survival was everything. At this time, duty, courage, obedience and constancy were paramount: the community came before the individual and the leader before all. In a number of settlements, Alba included, words considered 'weak' and 'selfish' were frowned on and gradually dropped out of use. It was these, often the words of poetry and emotion, that fell like rain onto the thirsty soil of the couple's imagination.

On the evening that Yash had stormed out of the seminar, they had been reading for a while when Cyrus looked up from his book and asked, "What's the difference between 'ignorant' and 'innocent'?"

Miouda shrugged. "Have you tried the dictionary?"

"No, I thought you might know."

"Well, 'ignorant' is not knowing something. But I haven't a clue what 'innocent' means. Go on, look it up."

Cyrus did as she suggested. "Damn!" he exclaimed, using one of the Long Dead words he had learned recently. "It's got masses of meanings: 'not hurtful; inoffensive; pure; harmless; guileless; simple-minded; ignorant of evil...' And I don't even understand half of them."

"The book you were reading might give us a clue," said Miouda, moving over to sit beside him. "Who did it say was innocent?"

Cyrus put an arm round her shoulders. "A child. This man said his adult sister was as innocent as a child. What do you think he meant?"

Miouda looked over at the dictionary and thought for a moment. "I suppose he was saying she was simple-minded, a bit stupid. None of the other meanings fit. I'm not sure about 'guileless', but you couldn't say a child was ignorant of evil, could you? A tiny baby, maybe; but not a child."

"No. And it's strange because the Long Dead seemed to think it was good to be innocent, good not to know about evil."

"They wouldn't last long in our world. Maybe that's why we don't use the word 'innocent' – it doesn't apply to us."

They sat in silence for a while, each wrapped up in their own thoughts. Eventually, Cyrus said, "There are other Long Dead words the Albans don't use any more, aren't there?"

"Yes. Words that don't fit in with our way of life. At least, that's what people like Yash say. He calls them 'baby words'."

"We used some of them back in Della Tallis. And they're here, in the books all around us."

She looked up into his face. "What words are you thinking of, Cyrus?"

He smiled. "Lots. But one especially. The Albans don't use it but I think you know what it is."

"Do I?"

"Yes. It begins with an L."

"You mean 'like'?"

"Sort of," he said, leaning over and kissing her forehead. "Except more so."

She sighed and snuggled up closer to him. "Ah! That one. We'd better not say it in case someone hears us and we get into trouble."

"Alright. But perhaps we can show it?"

"Yes," she said dreamily, "perhaps we can."

And there, in the darkening hall, Miouda discovered the

meaning of a word she had met only in books and on the lips of Cyrus. If she broke with custom and whispered it out loud, no one heard. The only witness to their movements was the carved and sightless head high on the beam above.

Ogg's men took two days to locate the Grozny. When they had done so, the oak-limbed Malik set out at once with a small escort to pay his allies a visit. Zed instincts were not easily suppressed and violent scuffles broke out when the Gurkovs appeared at the edge of the Grozny camp. Several men were injured before Jamshid brought his tribe to heel. The two Maliks sat down side by side on the trunk of a fallen tree and began to talk.

They felt a common sense of unease at what was going on. The alliance under Over-Malik Timur was a fine idea – but was it really under him? Jamshid was very proud. His defeat before the walls of Alba had upset as well as confused him. He reasoned, in his simplistic way, that since the failure could not be Timur's fault – nothing was – it must be someone else's. That it might be his own did not even occur to him. The responsibility, therefore, must somehow rest with Malika Xsani.

Ogg was thinking along similar lines. The delicious slaves Timur promised him had not shown up. As this couldn't be Timur's fault, whose was it? The only possibility was the mysterious Xsani whom he had met only in the blurry obscurity of the Timur ritual. Listening to Jamshid's account of the Alba expedition, all became clear. The Grozny operation had been agreed by Malika Xsani, Jamshid said, and –

151

"Who?" thundered Ogg, gasping and slapping a heavy hand on Jamshid's forearm.

Jamshid looked blank. "Who I say – Jamshid. Me." To make himself clear, he banged his chest. "This one."

"No, no, no!" cried Ogg. "Who said you should attack Alba?"

"Ah!" Jamshid nodded. "Timur order, Malika agree –"

"Malika?!" Ogg hammered his fists against the tree trunk they were sitting on. "Malik-a? A slave Malik?"

Jamshid frowned. "Timur say she good flabtoad, great flabtoad," he replied, annoyed by Ogg's interruption. "She clever, she hurt Jamshid very much. Look!" He pointed to the scars on his face left by Xsani's whip.

Ogg was not impressed. Slowly, step by step, he spelled things out for his fellow conspirator. Twice, what Timur had promised had not happened. There could be only one reason for this. Somehow this Xsani slave – "flabtoad," interrupted Jamshid – alright, flabtoad, had managed to trick the Over-Malik into trusting her.

"Slaves cannot be trusted," Ogg declared. "They are good only for games and breeding."

Jamshid, running his fingers over his scarred face, was still not wholly convinced. "Jamshid speak Timur," he muttered, groping for the right words. "Malika speak Timur. Malika strong."

Ogg leaned back thoughtfully. "Right, Jamshid, answer my questions. One, is Xsani a slave?"

"Maybe breeding slave?"

"Good. But when I met Timur, she did not show me her slave

face. She did not call herself 'Malika'. Why not, Jamshid? Why not?"

"Not know." Though this was the truth, Jamshid sensed the conversation was leading to another humiliation. He didn't have the wit or the skill to stop it.

"Malik Ogg is smart, Jamshid. He will explain. This Xsani slave is afraid of me! She hides from me! She knows I understand her trickery!" He pounded the tree again, this time in jubilation. "Is Ogg right, Jamshid?"

Jamshid had to admit the idea made sense. Moreover, to his relief, the great Gurkov did not tease him for his stupidity at allowing a woman to deceive him. Instead, Ogg declared the revelation to be proof of his own intelligence. Now he had found the source of their problems, he declared, he would tell Jamshid how they would solve them. The Grozny's new Malik, always more comfortable receiving orders than giving them, began to cheer up.

"Tomorrow morning," Ogg said, "I will bring the Gurkov here. Understand?"

Jamshid nodded. "First sun, Gurkov here."

"Good. The Gurkov and the Grozny will fight as one." The word 'fight' cheered Jamshid further and he jumped to his feet.

Ogg rose to stand beside him. "We will hunt the Kogon!"

"Hunt Kogon!" Jamshid echoed, waving his arms in excitement.

"Kill false Malika Xsani!"

"Kill Xsani!" Jamshid was almost dancing.

"Rescue Over-Malik Timur!"

Jamshid rolled his eyes in joy at the prospect. "Over-Malik Timur!" he gasped.

"With him at our head we will march on Alba and seize the Soterion! On to victory!" concluded Ogg with a tremendous flourish. Carried away with his own rhetoric, he clasped Jamshid to his trunk of a chest and heaved him off the ground.

Half-crushed in the arms of his new friend, Jamshid could only pant, "Sotion! Sotion! Sot-i-on!"

For several generations the Kogon Zeds had survived in a bitterly hostile world through guile and extreme watchfulness. Every fibre in Xsani's body warned her against trusting a man, especially one marked with a Z. It was only natural, therefore, that she should order her most skilful Eyes to keep the two Zed camps under constant surveillance. When Ogg set off to meet with Jamshid, she knew immediately. And when she heard the two men had been locked in discussions that ended in a fiery bonding, she suspected the worst.

Alright, she said to herself. If my allies want to play false, I will have to teach them a lesson they can never, ever forget.

8

King Yash

While Ogg and Jamshid were hatching their conspiracy, a Grozny party went out to look for food. The hunters returned dragging the bloody carcasses of three deer just as their leader's discussion was ending and Ogg was preparing to leave. To celebrate their new-found friendship, Jamshid asked his visitor to stay, enjoy the feast and afterwards join him in guarding the Grozny breeding slaves for a while. The temptation was too great for Ogg to resist.

The meat, roasted whole over enormous fires, was ready by late afternoon. The two Maliks each cut off large chunks and sat down again on their fallen tree trunk to chat over their planned coup. Women warriors, they agreed, would be easily swept aside. The prisoners they'd take would be useful for games and for boosting their tribes' numbers.

Ogg was boasting how many slave prisoners he would take, when he was interrupted by a commotion to their left.

Jamshid got up to investigate and returned with Giv. Neither Malik knew quite how to treat him. In Jamshid's eyes he was a worthy Captain of the tribe because he had saved the head of Timur. But as the men on the Gurkov embassy had noticed, Giv had changed. He spoke differently and had adopted some un-Grozny-like habits, such as cleaning his fingernails with a piece of wood rather than with his teeth. More worryingly, everyone knew he was a devoted servant of the Malika.

Ogg too was suspicious of Giv's relationship with Xsani. So when the emissary announced that the Malika wanted them at her base to discuss the forthcoming attack on Alba, Ogg told him to stay where he was for a moment. He had something important to discuss with his fellow Malik.

Taking Jamshid by the elbow, Ogg led him aside and asked, "Do you think he knows?"

"Knows what?"

Not for the first time, Ogg wondered why he was in partnership with such an oakhead. "Know about our plan to kill this Malika?"

Jamshid scratched himself and shook his head. "No."

"Right. We'll change our plan. She has invited us to talk with her, so we'll go – and kill her. Tonight."

"Kill," grinned Jamshid. "How?"

"Easy. Men against slaves is like killing deer, except slave killing is easier. They run slower."

Jamshid scratched his head again. "They not all flabtoads. Guards of no-stones," he said, reminding his ally of Xsani's eunuch bodyguard.

"Ha-ha-ha!" roared Ogg. "Jamshid is afraid of slaves and no-stones!"

"Jamshid not afraid!" The Grand Malik of the Grozny Zeds frowned angrily and clenched his fists.

"Good. We'll go there with one warrior each." In case Jamshid had not understood, Ogg explained, "You and one Grozny, and me and one Gurkov. Four big Zeds to fight slaves and no-stones. Fun, eh?"

"Big fun," agreed Jamshid. He called out to Giv, "Hey! Ogg and Jamshid come talk Malika, ok?"

"Good!" Giv called in reply.

Jamshid turned towards Ogg and slapped him on the back. "Jamshid say 'talk'! Ha-ha-ha! Giv not know! Ha-ha-ha!"

Once again, Ogg was astonished that he could have allied himself with such an ass.

The idea of recruiting Zeds had come to Sakamir while she was still back in Alba. To begin with, she had rejected it as too dangerous. It would work only if she found a second Timur. Without the protection of such a man – and it surely would be a man – she'd be as good as dead the moment a Zed set eyes on her. Even if there were a barbarian of sufficient intellect and ambition to recognise the importance of the Soterion, trusting him would be a tremendous risk.

She began to change her mind when she learned of Cyrus' anxiety about the missing head. Like him, she understood its power. She also reasoned that only a person of high intelligence would think of saving it and using it as a totem. In this she was only half right, of course: the humble Giv had saved the head – it took the astute Xsani to see its potential. Even when Sakamir left on patrol, she was not fully decided. It was the chanting of Jamshid's small force that finally persuaded her: someone, somewhere was exploiting the head's power. Whoever that person was, Sakamir told herself, they'd surely welcome her help.

She was right. She was also extremely fortunate to have fallen into the hands of the Kogon. Settled among them, she was surprised how at ease she felt. The cruelty, pain and brutality were strangely comforting. In the Zed world, life was stripped to its very barest, simplest essentials. The unwanted and even the awkward were eliminated without question. Abstract concepts like duty and loyalty were replaced by obedience enforced by punishment. To a greater extent even than among Constants, survival of the group was everything. With a few key exceptions, individuals did not exist. Sentiment was a laughable weakness.

Sakamir was attracted by another feature of Kogon life: the absence of men. She had always believed them crude and stupid, and had separated from her first copemate – an archer with more muscle than brain – shortly after the birth of Jalus and Poso. She had taken up with Yash because he seemed destined for leadership. Her hunch was right, though tolerating him had tested the limits of her patience. She longed to see the look on his face when, running a knife across his throat, she told him he was surplus to her requirements.

She looked forward to doing the same to Xsani as well. At that moment, in control of Alba and the Soterion, she would take that young Jinsha as her kumfort. It really was unfair of Xsani to keep such an attractive Zektiv all to herself.

But she was running ahead of herself. Jinsha could wait. For now she needed to watch the Malika and learn from her how to control Zeds. It was an art at which Xsani excelled – as she demonstrated in crushing Jamshid and Ogg's ill-fated coup.

It was dark by the time Giv led the two swaggering Maliks and their warrior escorts into Filna's central piazza. "There!" he announced, pointing to the balcony lit with flaming brands. "The Malika is waiting for you."

Ogg dug his elbow into Jamshid's ribs. "Malika!" he whispered. "Slave, more like!"

"Ha-ha!" chuckled Jamshid. "Big shock come!" He was right, though hardly in the manner he expected.

The four men, all clutching gut-rippers, followed Giv across the piazza and up the steps onto the balcony. As they reached the top, they heard the sound of light feet approaching behind them. They turned to see what it was – an elementary mistake in any combat. In this one, it was fatal.

As the Zeds raised their clumsy weapons to fend off the Kogon spears advancing up the steps, Xsani's eunuch bodyguard attacked. The two escort warriors were slain immediately. After a brief struggle, Ogg and Jamshid were disarmed and pinned to the ground. Xsani, flanked by Jinsha, Yalisha, Tarangala and Sakamir, advanced until she was standing directly above them.

"Snivelling slave!" cried Ogg, wrestling unsuccessfully to free himself. "You have cheated the Over-Malik Timur. I will pound you to a mess of flesh!"

A smile played along Xsani's lips and she raised a light-brown eyebrow. "Tho, I wath right. You and thith motht thupid dumbman have come here to kill me."

"Oh tho clev –" began Ogg before the first lash of the Malika's whip stopped his mouth and left a broad cut across his top lip. A further six blows fell. When she had finished, Xsani bent down and wiped the thongs of her whip clean on his loincloth before neatly tucking her weapon back into her sleeve.

"Thothe are from Timur, our mathter," she announced, gazing at the lattice of lacerations that had been Ogg's face. One lash had fallen directly over his left eye, slicing through the eyelid and the soft flesh of the cheekbone below. If he did see again, it would only ever be with one eye.

"He ith not pleathed, Ogg. You have betrayed him."

The Malik of the Gurkov Zeds groaned and, with a supreme effort, moaned, "No, slave! You have betrayed him."

From the direction of the steps came a low hiss and Ogg mentally braced himself for a fresh assault. He would die, he told himself, rather than submit to this slave. Xsani thought for a moment. She wanted Ogg as an obedient living ally, not a dead one. Without him the Gurkov would be impossible to control and the coalition would fall apart. A subtler approach was called for.

"Let uth thee all the dumbman," she said, signalling to Tarangala. As the Zektiv reached for Ogg's loincloth, he shivered uncontrollably.

"You have the knife, Jintha?"

Xsani's kumfort held out a long blade. Ogg groaned as it

glinted orange and blood red in the flames of the torches. The Malika looked at her people gathered on the steps. "Thall we thtart?" she asked. The women hissed their eager approval.

Ogg turned his head violently from side to side, flecking with drops of blood the bodies of the men who held him.

"Come forward, Jintha," said Xsani, "and we thall begin." Ogg groaned again, louder this time. Then, to his astonishment, nothing happened. Instead, there was a great deal of noise and scuffling to his left. Surely not? But yes, it was Jamshid! Jinsha had begun with the once-Grand Malik of the Grozny Zeds.

When it was over, Xsani came back to Ogg. "Dumbman Jamthid twithe betrayed Over-Malik Timur," she explained. "He hath paid twithe. You betrayed him oneth. But you theduthed Jamthid into rebellion, tho you altho will pay twithe."

Ogg was defeated. Shining with sweat and quivering like a reed, he begged for mercy. At first, the Malika pretended to be reluctant to listen, but eventually she relented and Ogg was led, half-blind, to the sty. Amid the smoke he was visited again by Timur. The ghostly Over-Malik confirmed that he had chosen Jamshid's punisment and would not hesitate to order the same for Ogg if he ever dared step out of line again.

He never did.

Two days later, Giv took Jamshid back to the Grozny camp. There, the former Malik was stripped of his stinking furs and made to stand before the whole tribe. This, they were told as they paraded before him, was what happened to those who defied the Over-Malik. The first few Zeds stared at Jamshid's injuries in astonished disbelief. Then one of them pointed and began to snigger. Those who followed chuckled out loud, and before long the entire tribe was hooting with laughter and yelling, "Jamshid flabtoad! Jamshid flabtoad!" at the top of their voices.

After the noise had subsided, Giv announced that Timur had made him the new Malik of the Grozny. He immediately appointed four Captains and cemented his authority by breaking the fingers of two men who wondered whether he had seen enough winters to qualify as a Malik. The submission of the Grozny was completed the next night when the entire tribe was brought to Filna's piazza and, in a special ceremony, introduced to the Timur totem and Malika Xsani.

This time the blackened head was suspended from a window above the balcony. Giv, standing in the shadows behind it, spoke with total conviction: "I am Timur, the mighty Zed who lives for ever. Look on me and tremble, ratbrains!

"Grozny, Gurkov and Kogon – all Zeds are one under me. Malika Xsani knows my will. Follow her, antheads, and I will be with you.

"Now, tell me who I am!"

With one voice the Grozny howled, "Timur! Timur! Timur!" until Xsani quietened them down in order to lead a pledge of loyalty.

"Mighty Timur," responded the mob, "who lives for ever, you and the Malika are one."

When Jamshid died of blood poisoning two days later, his death was seen as a sign. It was obvious, wasn't it? All those foolish enough to challenge Timur or Xsani were bound to perish in humiliating agony.

The loyalty pledge was repeated with the Gurkov the following night. Xsani's triumph was complete. She controlled a coalition of three powerful Zed tribes and had an alliance with a former Alban who would open the settlement's gates to the Zed coalition. Even if Sakamir betrayed her, Xsani reckoned she had sufficient force at her command to storm the walls. But of course the whole operation would be so much easier if her guest did not play false…

"We will attack at the netht full moon. You will not betray me, will you Thakamir?" she asked on the day her visitor left to return to Alba. She knew she could not expect an honest answer, but hoped the manner of the response might reveal something.

Sakamir's unsmiling stare gave nothing away. She nodded and said in a flat, expressionless tone, "You can trust me, Xsani. You may not believe me, but when you reach Alba you will find all I have told you is true."

In this she was correct. She had outlined the paths taken by Alban patrols so the Zeds could avoid them as they advanced. This might not be necessary, she had revealed, because her copemate Yash should have cut the number of patrols to a minimum. She also outlined Alban fighting techniques and gave Xsani a map of the settlement showing where the gates and important buildings were. She even marked the position of the Ghasar correctly. It could do no harm, she told herself, because the Malika would not last long after Alba had fallen.

The two women parted with scarcely a flicker of acknowledgement. They were too clever, too suspicious even to pretend there was anything like friendship between them. Quite rightly, each suspected the other of playing a double game for sole possession of the Soterion. For the time being, co-operation was mutually beneficial. The situation would not last, of course. In the final battle, only one would conquer.

The Albans accepted Cyrus' relationship with Miouda more readily than he had expected. Back home in Della Tallis, couples usually stayed together until death. The Albans saw things differently. Intense personal relationships were discouraged as they got in the way of loyalty to the community and the Emir. This made the early death of a partner – a common occurrence, especially in childbirth – easier to handle. By the age of fifteen or sixteen, Alban women had normally had at least one child before returning to military and agricultural duties. They often changed copemate at the same time, as Sakamir had done.

Miouda and her copemate of three years were childless. Both accepted their relationship had burned out, so there were no objections when she took to remaining in the Ghasar overnight with Cyrus. Sammy said they suited one another like bow and arrow, and he was surprised they'd taken so long to get together. Even Bahm told Cyrus he found the new friendship "just as it ought to be, considering". Cyrus didn't ask him what 'considering' meant.

Unsurprisingly, the only adverse comment came from Yash. Was it right, he demanded, very loudly and very publicly, for an Alban to have a copemate from outside the settlement? He wasn't sure, but he didn't like it. He also told Miouda she was foolish to have a relationship with someone near the end of his life, and he asked Cyrus – only half in jest – whether he was enjoying Alba's generous hospitality. Cyrus found this hostility, like so much of the Emir's recent behaviour, hard to fathom. Since Miouda was considered one of the best-looking women in the community, he put it down partly to jealousy.

The only other stain on the couple's happiness was an ominous feeling that it wouldn't last. He couldn't put a finger on it, Cyrus said one evening as they lay together in the thickening twilight, but he sensed something barbaric was gathering its dark strength to strike.

Miouda raised herself onto one elbow. "It's to do with Yash's strange behaviour, and Sakamir going missing, isn't it? And probably the business of Timur's head."

Cyrus nodded. "I'm sure they're linked."

"Remember Padmar's warning?"

"Yes. She was right, wasn't she? I suppose, when you think about it, there's something in what Bahm says." He lay back and waved a hand at the piles of books. "These are the solution – and the problem. Before we found the Soterion, we believed it would be the answer to everything. It'd take us back to the time of the Long Dead and we'd live in peace and happiness."

"And write poems," said Miouda, "and make pictures and take those P-H things – what're they called?"

"Photographs." He pronounced the P and H at the beginning and end of the word separately, not as Fs. "But it's not like that, is it? The Long Dead may have done amazing things – driving in cars, flying in the sky – but we now know they weren't so different from us, were they?"

"Mmm, but they didn't have Zeds," said Miouda.

"No, but they had wars. *The Odyssey* characters are fighting all the time. There's something else. We – Roxanne, you, me, Sammy – we thought book knowledge was simply a way to a better world. We didn't see the power Padmar warned us about. The quest for domination is stronger than spears and arrows.

"Take the Salvation Project," he continued. "It's like a large and lovely flower, dripping with more honey than we can imagine. Bees from all around are desperate to find it. Some want to carry away the honey and distribute it far and wide; others plan to keep it for themselves. Timur, Padmar, maybe Sakamir, Yash and others we don't know, they are these selfish bees."

Miouda lay down again and snuggled close, resting her head on his shoulder. "So we're the nice bees, are we?" she said quietly, her lips against his ear. "And when we get the honey, we'll be the powerful ones."

Cyrus laughed quietly. "For a while, maybe. But we're vulnerable and the selfish bees are jealous. They won't leave us in peace for long, I'm sure they won't." Running his hand over the smooth skin of her back, he pulled her even closer. "So we'd better enjoy the sweetness while we can."

"Got it!" cried Sammy, jumping up and doing a little dance. "Look, Cyrus, I've found a picture of one. I understand what they are now."

The other students looked up and smiled. Typical Sammy!

He was always so full of energy and enthusiasm, continually coming up with some amazing discovery from the time of the Long Dead. What was it this time?

Cyrus got up and walked over to see what his friend was up to. "Yes, Sammy? Got what?"

"Those things you called 'trays' when we brought them up from the vault. You remember, those things over there." He pointed to a pile of five metal slabs gathering dust in a corner of the hall. "They ain't trays. They're computers."

All the other students except Yash had crowded round the book Sammy had open on the floor before him.

"There you are," he said, pointing at an array of photographs and diagrams arranged on a double-page spread. "It tells you at the top what it's all about: 'The De-velop-ment of the Computer.' They're amazing!"

"It says here," he went on, "that one of these things can have a million books in it! A million, all squashed into one box. And you can write new books with it. Fantastic!"

As he was talking, Miouda had gone over to the pile of computers and returned with one. She laid it on the floor next to the book Sammy had been looking at. He leaned across and opened the lid to reveal the keyboard and screen.

"Dah-dah!" he said triumphantly. "A computer! This kind is called a – hang on a moment…" He ran his finger over the open pages as he read. "Yeah, a … laptop or a notebook. Here's the picture of one. There were loads of other kinds."

"So where are the millions of books, Sam?" asked one of the twelve-year-olds.

"Inside, I suppose. I'll research about it, but I think they show up on this shiny bit." He pointed to the screen.

"Go on, Sam," said another of the students. "See if you can make them show up."

Sammy exhaled loudly and looked across at the Emir. "That's where the problem comes. You need electricity to make these things go, and we ain't got any. That's why I said maybe a patrol could go and get one of them panels –"

"No!" shouted Yash from the other side of the hall. "You heard me last time, didn't you Sammy? No patrols. I'm not wasting my archers on a daft plan to make a million books come out of a box."

Sammy sighed heavily. "Ok, ok! Sorry, Yash."

"Right. So drop it, Sammy. You're a guest here – and don't you forget it!"

The Emir's unreasonable outburst ended the conversation, and the students began to drift back to what they had been doing before the interruption. The awkward silence was broken by Miouda, who had been examining the laptop's keyboard.

"What do you think S P stands for?" she asked.

"Six People?" one of the twelve-year-olds suggested.

"Why're you asking?" inquired Cyrus. He stooped down, slipping an arm affectionately round Miouda's shoulders.

"Someone's scratched them onto the computer," she said, pointing to the two letters etched into the aluminium beside the keyboard. "Soterion Property?"

"Oh no!" said Cyrus, his voice suddenly hoarse with excitement. "I bet it's not that, Miouda. I think it's what we've been looking for: how about S and P standing for 'Salvation Project'?"

He looked up to find everyone staring at him in astonishment. "That must be it," he said slowly, thinking out loud. "The books contain everything the Long Dead knew. I imagine they took some time to make. But when they were dying out, the Long Dead didn't have any time. No time to make new books, anyway. So maybe, as they were working on the Salvation Project, they wrote down what they were doing inside one of these computers."

He paused to allow the others to take in the significance of his argument. "Yes, that makes sense," said Miouda. "It must be why they left the computers in the Soterion, alongside the books."

She stood up. "Here you are, Emir," she said, picking up the computer and holding it out towards Yash. "It looks like we've found the Salvation Project."

Sammy came to stand next to her. "But we can't read it until we get electricity."

"Which means we need a patrol to go and get one of those panel things," said Cyrus, standing between his two friends

For a moment, Yash said nothing. Then he rose and walked up to Miouda. "Clever," he said slowly, taking the laptop from her. "Very clever. You may be right. On the other hand, how do we know Sammy didn't scratch those letters?"

Moving over to where Miouda had found it, he carefully replaced the laptop on top of the pile. "Let's leave it here, shall we? I think we need to see what happens before we do anything."

Cyrus was seething. "'See what happens', Yash? What in the name of Alba do you mean?"

Yash strode angrily over to him. "Oh! Don't you understand, Mister Clever Man?" he shouted, standing so close that his breath ruffled Cyrus' hair. "I thought you understood everything? Well, let me explain. 'See what happens' means leave it alone – got it?"

"I get that, Yash," said Cyrus steadily. "But it's not right."

"Oh really? I'm the Emir and I'll say what we'll do with that laptop thing, and when we do it. Understand? And if you challenge me, Cyrus, I'll break you. You're not as important as you were, are you? Lots of people can read now. If I were you, Outsider, I'd be very, very careful what you say."

That evening Cyrus, Miouda and Sammy met together to decide what to do. For whatever reason, Yash had clearly taken against all three of them. In one thing he was right, too – a number of Albans were reading well. Cyrus no longer had a monopoly on learning. If Yash decided to do away with him – and Sammy and Miouda as well – Soterion study would be seriously hampered but it wouldn't stop altogether. As Yash warned, they had to take great care.

They discussed the possibility of going behind Yash's back and smuggling a solar panel into Alba without his knowing. Getting out would be easy, said Miouda. The problem would be getting back in. Their absence without permission would be noted, and bringing a large panel in through the gates or over the walls without the guards noticing would be almost impossible.

"But not totally impossible," said Cyrus. "And we mightn't

170

need to sneak it in. Listen. How about this?"

He and Sammy could slip out easily enough. They would take the SP laptop with them, find a panel and get it to make electricity. Once the computer was full of electricity – however that worked – they would see what was inside it. The Salvation Project, probably. They would come back with the panel and show everyone how they had found the key to abolishing the Death Month. Not even Yash would dare punish them for that, would he?

Miouda was sceptical. She certainly didn't want Cyrus and Sammy going off into Zed territory without her. And where would they find this panel? For reasons of security and infection, the Alba settlement had been deliberately set up a long way from Long Dead towns. None of the three knew the surrounding area well and they might search for several moons – months, corrected Sammy – before they found a panel. Even then, they wouldn't know how to make it work…

Cyrus interrupted her. Yes, it was a dangerous mission. But he had done this sort of thing before, and the alternative was to leave the hope of salvation gathering dust in the corner of the Ghasar. And if Miouda wanted to come with them, that'd be wonderful. But it would be dangerous.

"Hardly more than staying here with Yash in the mood he's in," she replied.

In the end, they agreed to investigate further before reaching a firm decision. Sammy would chat to those who had been on patrol and find out where the nearest Long Dead town was; Miouda would learn how computers worked and how they could be filled with electricity; Cyrus would research solar panels. They'd meet up when they had done their research and decide whether to go ahead with the mission.

The meeting never took place. Long before they had finished gathering their information, Cyrus' relationship with the Emir took a grave turn for the worse.

Two issues widened the gulf between the two men. The first was that Yash, against Cyrus' advice, had been experimenting with wine-making. Having located vines growing on the other side of the mountain, he had baskets full of grapes carried to a hidden location on the terraces where they were crushed and left in a water tank to ferment. Bahm, who'd seen what was going on and told Cyrus, said Yash intended to keep the process secret so he could present the new drink to the community as a novelty, a gift from their Emir.

The second matter was more serious. For some time Yash had shown great interest in a book about the history of ancient Rome. "It shows how settlements change," he said when asked why it was so interesting. "This Rome, you see, was like Alba."

Cyrus, who knew little of Long Dead history, didn't see the significance of the remark until too late. His suspicions were first aroused one evening when he overheard the Emir talking to a group of his archer friends after class.

"And what happened," Yash was explaining, "is that instead of having to choose a new Emir every time one died, they had a different system. The leader was called a 'king' or an 'emperor'. When they died, their son – nearly always was a son, not a daughter – took over their job. Simple, eh? It was called 'monarchy' – 'herenary monarchy', or something like that. A really good idea."

A couple of days after that, Yash told Cyrus that Jalus and Poso needed extra classes in the morning because they were 'special'. When Cyrus asked what 'special' meant, he was told he'd find out soon enough.

The answer came at the next monthly assembly of the Konnels. As he had done since Yash's election, Cyrus attended as an honoured Outsider. At the start of the meeting, the Emir stood up and said he had a very important announcement to make. He reminded them – in case they didn't know – that he had been studying hard and as a consequence of his labours he was well educated, very well educated. He had been reading how groups like the Albans were governed in Long Dead times. The best way was by 'herenary monarchy' – and he'd decided that was how Alba would be governed from now on.

"Meaning?" asked one of the older Konnels, a black-haired woman expected to enter her Death Month at any moment.

Yash looked around, grinning. "Well, the most obvious thing is that I'm not going to be an Emir much longer. I'll be a king. Your king. King Yash!"

Murmurs of surprise and incomprehension ran through the hall. Eventually a single voice cut through the hubbub. "No, that's completely wrong, Yash. I'm sorry, but you can't do it. Constants everywhere govern themselves. Choosing our leaders is part of being a Constant. We do not have hereditary kings."

It was Cyrus. As Yash looked at him, his eyes narrowed and

his lip lifted in a sneer. "Don't say I haven't warned you, Cyrus," he began. "And this time you've gone too far."

At that moment, the door of the Ghasar flew open and a guard from the Soterion Gate ran into the hall. "Emir!" she gasped. "Emir, you must come to the gate now. It's really urgent!"

9

Sakamir

"Sakamir! Sakamir!" The word scuttled about the settlement like a breeze, rustling round the square, pushing through windows and doors, and climbing the terraces above. "Sakamir is back! She's escaped, escaped from the Zeds!"

A crowd gathered in the square to watch in astonishment and admiration as Yash supported his long-lost copemate up the street from the gate and into the Emiron. Her shift was dishevelled and torn. She was still wearing her sandals, though she limped painfully. What attracted most attention was the tattoo: there, burned into her forehead, was the unmistakeable brand of a Zed.

Standing on the end of the square nearest the Ghasar, Cyrus watched with a heavy heart. He had never liked Sakamir, but to have been captured by the Zeds... He wouldn't wish that on anybody. He knew only too well what she must have endured. Roxanne, who had been through the dreadful experience herself, had spared him the grisly details. But she had said enough, and he shuddered at the thought of it. The brutality, starvation, rape, humiliation... Sakamir would probably never fully recover. He felt guilty, too, because the patrol had been his idea. Nevertheless, he couldn't help wondering how she'd managed to get away.

His mind recalled that fateful morning in Della Tallis when he and his best friend Navid had hurried to the barricades to beat off a Zed attack. Except it had not been an attack, but Roxanne struggling to reach safety before she was torn to pieces by Grozny dogs. A refugee with a Z tattoo. It was he who had saved her by persuading Taja to shoot the dogs. Staring over the palisade, even at a distance, he had noticed something different about the refugee staggering towards him...

He remembered hauling her over the barrier and lying her down on the grass. In his mind's eye he saw again the smooth, damaged skin and the pleading green eyes. She had indeed been exceptional. For her sake, if for no other reason, he had pledged to carry the Soterion Mission through. As she had once put it, reason, learning, art, truth and beauty had to triumph – or what was the point in anything?

He was dragged into the present by a wet nose snuffling against his leg. Corby! "Hello, old boy," he said, patting the dog's broad flank. "Where's your master, eh?"

"Here!" Sammy, who had watched the arrival of Sakamir from the other side of the square, had made his way round to Cyrus. "So she's back. What do you make of it?"

"I'm pleased for her. Why?"

"Nothing really. Just odd the Zeds didn't take her shoes, isn't it?"

It was an acute observation, and Cyrus understood immediately what it might mean. But this wasn't the place to talk. "Sammy, something really important happened just before Sakamir arrived. We need to talk about it – somewhere we won't be overheard."

"Up the terraces?"

"Ok."

They talked as they climbed, Cyrus explaining Yash's monarchy idea and how he'd reacted when Cyrus challenged him. He was sure things were coming to a climax, but he still couldn't fit the pieces of the puzzle together. Had Sammy any idea what linked Yash's behaviour and Sakamir's absence?

Sammy paused before answering. "Well – stop me if I've got it wrong – but why didn't Timur and them Zeds kill Roxanne?"

"Because he was fascinated by her, like we all were."

"Yes. She were special looking and special in her person. But there was something else, Cyrus, wasn't there? Something Timur wanted."

"You mean the Soterion."

"Exactly. Timur found out about it from her. She was the key to the door, and he wasn't stupid enough to go throwing it –"

"I know, I know," interrupted Cyrus. "That's just what I hope isn't true. I don't want to hear Roxanne's story over again." Sammy, looking his friend straight in the eye, said nothing. "Ok, so you reckon Sakamir survived because she handed over information about the Soterion?"

"Can't see no other way, can you?"

Cyrus sat on the top terrace and considered the implications of what they were saying. He knew the Zeds used captured Constant women for entertainment before killing them. Only those young enough for breeding slaves were left alive. Sakamir was in her final year, so how had she survived if not by passing on information?

"See what I mean?" said Sammy after a while. "It was them shoes that set me thinking."

"Sure." Cyrus frowned. "It's strange she was allowed to keep them. They tortured Roxanne to get information out of her. I wonder if they did the same to Sakamir…"

"Dunno. Hope not. She actually chose to go out on that patrol, didn't she? She said she went looking for the Zeds because she wanted to destroy Timur's head."

"What if destroying it was actually the last thing she was planning to do? I don't like where this is leading us, Sammy." He paused for a moment before adding, "And she's fascinated by the Soterion."

"Not as much as Yash."

"That's because she's more subtle, Sammy. She doesn't want to give the game away."

He shrugged. "This is all getting pretty complicated, isn't it Cyrus?"

"Yes, and worrying. A while ago, I dreamed about what might be happening – a sort of nightmare fantasy. If we're right, it seems to be coming true. Here's what I think's going on.

"Yash and Sakamir – acting together – plan to take over the

Soterion and its Salvation Project. It'll make them and their children all-powerful. They know the Albans won't let them do this, so Sakamir risks her life to get Grozny support. Meanwhile, Yash weakens Alba's defences and tries to increase his power by becoming king. Remember what he said when we asked permission to try and make the laptop work?"

"He said we had to wait to see what happens."

"Exactly. Wait until he's taken over. So … Sakamir returns from the Grozny. Somehow she's got their new leader on her side. All's ready for a Zed-backed coup. Any day now…"

Sammy let out a low whistle. "And Padmar's warning comes true. Sounds like a story from a book… You honestly think it might be happening like that?"

"Could be. It makes sense of what's going on, doesn't it?"

"Most of it. But not that Zed attack where I got injured."

"You're right. I don't get that either. Perhaps Sakamir can explain – I'll ask her if I get a chance. We've got to watch our backs, though. I was wrong to challenge Yash openly when he said he was going to be king. We can't do much on our own. Strength will come through numbers – we have to build up a group of supporters. In the meantime, we must appear to go along with things. I'll start by apologising to Yash."

Cyrus never made his apology. Returning from the terraces, he was arrested by a group of archers. He recognised several of them from Yash's former patrol. Sammy was incensed by the move and got into a fight with one of the guards, and when Corby joined in, sinking his teeth into the man's leg, the situation threatened to get nasty. It calmed down thanks to Cyrus personally restraining Sammy and getting him to call off his dog. In the end, the impetuous young man was fortunate to have got away with nothing more than a bleeding nose and a burning sense of injustice.

There was no gaol in Alba, just a stone detention centre in which prisoners were held before trial. To avoid wasting time and effort with long-term incarceration, sentences were decided swiftly and punishment handed out almost immediately: flogging, exile or – rarely – death.

Sitting in the dark of the cell, Cyrus speculated on what his punishment might be. It depended what he was charged with. The archers who seized him said he had challenged the authority of the Emir, but that authority did not extend to taking over the government and ruling single-handed, surely? It went against all Constant traditions. He wondered whether an assembly of Konnels would consider this an adequate defence.

He hadn't been alone for long when the bars of the door drew back and the cell was flooded with late afternoon sunlight. A moment later a figure appeared, silhouetted against the glare. Temporarily blinded, Cyrus didn't recognise who it was. But the voice he knew instantly.

"Hello Cyrus! I'm sorry to find you in here."

Sakamir.

"Just the person I was thinking about!" he said, rising to his feet as he searched for the right words. "I feel bad, Sakamir. That patrol was my idea…"

"I chose to lead it, Cyrus."

She was hardly recognisable from the hobbling woman he had seen in the square earlier in the day. She had combed her brown hair straight and exchanged her torn and tattered gown for a clean white one. Telling the guard to leave the door ajar so they had some light, she walked carefully to the wooden bench opposite the entrance and sat down. She signalled for Cyrus to sit beside her.

"Well," she began, turning her thin face full towards him, "I'm back."

He lifted his gaze from the dark, expressionless eyes to the raw scar on her forehead. It was real alright. Whatever else may or may not have been done to her, the branding would have been excruciating.

"It was not a pleasant experience," she said. "As Roxanne must have told you."

Cyrus winced inwardly at the reminder. "How did you manage it? Getting away, I mean."

"I was very, very fortunate. They let me live so I could teach their future leaders. 'Teach', they called me. I'd told them I could read, you see."

"We're talking about the Grozny, yes?"

"Just the Grozny."

"Ah! So there are Grozny Zeds who can read?"

When she shook her head, a lock of fair hair fell across her forehead, obscuring her tattoo. She pushed it aside quickly. "Not really. I explained a few letters, that's all."

He wanted to ask so many questions. How had she been captured? What had happened to Potr? What were the Grozny like? Did she remember any of their names? Anything to test her story. Lowering his gaze to those deep-set and impenetrable eyes, he wondered whether she sensed this.

"I have come here to tell you that you're a free man," she announced.

The sudden change of subject caught him off guard and, in a gesture of gratitude, he reached out and took her hand in his. "Thank you, Sakamir!"

"You are still too precious to be locked away." Having briefly responded to the pressure of his touch, she drew back her hand. "I told Yash to let you go. He can be rather foolish at times, though he regrets what he did."

"He regrets that king business?"

She hesitated for an instant. "I'm not sure, Cyrus. What I mean is that he's sorry for ordering your arrest. I wanted to give you the news myself."

"Why?"

"Because, as I said, I value you. And I knew you'd be the only person to really understand what I've been through. The pain. The loneliness." She swallowed as if holding back tears. "But at least we carried out our mission."

"So they'd taken the head, had they? And you destroyed it?"

"Almost. You were right, Cyrus, they did cut off Timur's head. But they didn't guard it very carefully; I heard that wolves carried it off and ate it."

"Thank goodness!" He wanted to ask why, if the head was lost, the Grozny who attacked Alba had chanted about it? He decided that would be too direct. "And Potr? I suppose they killed him straight off?"

"When we were captured. He died defending me."

"I'm sorry." He tried a more direct question. "Roxanne said, apart from Timur, the worst were Jumshid and Jamshid. Did you see them?"

"Jamshid, yes. But not the other one. There was also someone called Giv. Horrible, truly horrible."

"I can imagine. Who's their new leader?"

She replied without hesitation, "Jamshid. A brute – but not clever like Timur."

"Do they know about the Soterion?"

"They remembered something Timur had told them – and I confirmed it." Cyrus started. "Don't worry, I told them Bahm had burned the books because he didn't like the new-fangled ideas they contained. One of the Grozny – Giv, I think it was – said he remembered seeing smoke from behind the walls when he was collecting Timur's head. After what I'd said, they assumed it was from the book burning."

"Lucky, eh?"

"Very. Not that they understood what the Soterion really is. They're too stupid. They lost interest after they learned it'd been destroyed and moved on towards sunhigh to find an easier target. That's when I escaped."

"They were headed south?"

"South, yes. I remember the word."

"Your escape – was it difficult?"

She closed her eyes and sighed heavily. "Sorry, Cyrus, but it'll have to wait. You of all people must realise how tired I am.

Absolutely shattered." She stood up and walked slowly towards the door. "I look forward to getting back to your classes, by the way. When my strength returns. I've a lot to catch up on, haven't I?"

"You're clever, Sakamir," he said, rising to his feet. "It won't take you long."

By the door, she paused and turned to face him. "A group of words have been churning around in my head ever since I left. I want you to tell me what they mean and how to write them."

"Of course. What are they?"

"Hairy liaise marry clog."

He frowned and shook his head. "Not a clue. We'll have to use the dictionary. Where did you read them?"

"Oh, somewhere. I can't remember. And I don't suppose you've come across a picture of a dumb ... a man with a large yellow hat?"

"No."

"No matter." She put her hand on the door and pushed it fully open. "Thank you for listening to me, Cyrus. And thank you for understanding. As I said, Alba needs people like you."

"And thank you for freeing me," Cyrus called as she disappeared into the glare.

After she had gone, he sat down heavily on the bench. Well! What was he to make of all that? Apart from one or two obviously contrived moments, she had been so matter-of-fact. The contrast with Roxanne after her escape could hardly be greater. And so many loose ends. Why had she persuaded Yash to free him? If Timur's head had been lost, why had the warband used it in their chant? What did 'just the Grozny' mean? Why didn't she want to tell him about her escape? And where on earth did 'hairy liaise marry clog' and a man in a large yellow hat come from?

Instead of making things clearer, Sakamir's unexpected visit had left him more confused than ever.

On his way to the Ghasar, Cyrus was stopped several times by people telling him how pleased they were he'd been freed. He thanked them and said his detention had been a mistake, a simple misunderstanding. He decided there was nothing to be gained by openly challenging Yash at this stage.

Sammy didn't agree. He caught sight of Cyrus as he was nearing the hall and rushed towards him with outstretched arms. Corby, as delighted as his master, bounded along beside him.

"Cyrus!" he cried, throwing his arms round him like a child. "You didn't half have me worried! When I heard you'd been let out, I ran quick as I could to check it with my own eyes." He paused to gulp in a breath of air. "So what're we going to do about Yash, then?"

"Shh! Not so, loud, Sammy!"

"Eh? Come on! You're not going to let him get away with it, are you?"

Cyrus looked round anxiously. "Not here. I'll explain everything when we're indoors."

He found Miouda waiting for him in the hall. After a tearful reunion, she sat cross-legged on the floor while he ran through what had happened at the Konnels' meeting and during his detention. His conversation with Sakamir, he confessed, had left him totally confused. Yes, she had definitely been with the Zeds. They had almost certainly captured her and made her one of their own – the horrible Z brand was genuine enough. She knew the name of the Grozny's new leader as well – it was someone Roxanne had mentioned.

Even so, her story didn't quite add up. Accompanied by Potr, she had gone looking for the Grozny; she had been held by them for a while before returning, alone, in a far better state than might have been expected. She had then arranged for Cyrus to be released because he was 'still too precious'. What did the others make of it?

Sammy thought the whole thing extremely suspicious. He wanted Cyrus to come out in the open and challenge Yash. He was sure most Albans would support him.

Miouda urged caution. Whatever benefits Cyrus might have brought the community, she reminded him that he remained an Outsider. It would be a mistake to underestimate the Albans' loyalty to their Emir, she insisted. Obedience had been drilled into them since birth. Besides, the return of Sakamir had strengthened his hand. Though not popular before her disappearance, she was now seen as a bit of a hero. A 'second Roxanne', one or two women were calling her. The Albans would turn against their Emir and his copemate only on hearing the strongest evidence against them.

"And that's just what we haven't got," said Cyrus. "But we can't do nothing. At present Sakamir is untouchable, so we'll focus on Yash. As Emir, he's the strongest member of the partnership. But his impetuosity and lack of subtlety also makes him the weakest link. I shouldn't think his king idea will go down well when it gets out. I can't imagine what Bahm'll say about it!"

"Bahm don't like anything to change," said Sammy. "He wants every day to be yesterday."

Cyrus smiled. "I'll have a chat with him tomorrow, sound him out."

"And I'll tell you something else," Sammy added. "He don't like Yash making that wine stuff."

"Good," said Cyrus. "That's one thing we agree on, at least. I can start there."

The three of them sat talking until it was quite dark. When Sammy eventually left for his dormitory, Miouda went to the door to see him off. Cyrus joined her on the threshold. All was still. Even the crickets seemed to have taken the night off, and under a bright gibbous moon the settlement lay black-and-white before them like a photograph.

Miouda rested her head against his shoulder. "How quiet it all is!" she said softly. "It's like everything, even the buildings and walls, are asleep."

"A Long Dead poet wrote about that."

"Who was it?"

"I can't remember. I only glanced at the poem. It was about a bridge, I think." He wrapped an arm around her. "The poet mentioned that 'God' thing. I wish someone would explain to me exactly what it means."

"Me too. But I don't think the Long Dead had a very clear idea. As far as I can see, it meant whatever they wanted."

"Like the moon? God is the moon!"

"Maybe. And the moon is also God." She raised her eyes above the grey shadow of the walls. "In three days the God moon will be full and bright."

They stood for a few moments before Cyrus added, "A full moon's special, isn't it? It's when things happen."

"Not this time, I hope." She shuddered and held him tighter. "Come on, it's getting chilly. Let's go back inside."

The next day started with ominous normality. After a quick bite to eat, Cyrus gave an extra lesson to Jalus and Poso, as Yash had demanded. He then joined Miouda for work on the terraces before finishing the morning with military training in the square. Sammy, whose accuracy with a bow was still well below that of the Albans, spent his time shooting arrows at a target by the Soterion Gate. As usual, the students turned up for classes shortly after sunhigh. Yash sat down without a word and continued reading his history book. He was very fidgety, Cyrus noticed, and frequently glanced around the room. Clearly eager to be elsewhere, he left early.

When the classes were over, Miouda went to see a friend and Cyrus set out to visit a sick child in one of the junior dormitories. His path led him across the square. As he approached the well, he noticed a figure sitting on the ground with their back against the surrounding wall. It was Jannat.

"Hello," he said as he approached. "What're you doing, Jannat? You ok?"

She raised her head and looked towards him with unfocussed eyes. "Lovely!" she said, pronouncing the word as if her tongue was too big for her mouth. A dribble of saliva ran down her lip onto her chest.

Alarmed, Cyrus squatted down and took her hand. "What is it, Jannat? What's the matter?"

"I've been drinking Yash's wine!" she slurred with exaggerated care. "It's lovely!"

"Lovely? You seem in a bad way."

"No, Cyrus! Wine makes you do amazing things!" She grinned salaciously. "Wanna know a secret?"

"Go on."

"I been with Sakamir!"

"You what?"

"Shh! It's a secret. I been with Sakamir on the terraces." She lowered her head. After taking an intense interest in Cyrus' feet for a moment, she lifted it again and asked, "You want to kiss me too?"

"I don't think so, Jannat." He got up and stood looking down at her. "There's something wrong with you. You're not yourself."

She didn't reply. After Cyrus had repeated the question and still received no answer, he knelt beside her again. To his astonishment, he found she was sound asleep.

Instead of going to the dormitory, he returned to the Ghasar and opened the dictionary. A ... B ... C ... D ... yes, there it was. 'Drunk, adj. '. Fascinated, Cyrus read the entry before turning to the encyclopaedia and looking up 'alcohol'.

As he was reading, he became aware of a throbbing noise

outside. He ignored it and continued to the end of the article. Miouda came hurrying into the hall as he was finishing.

"Have you heard, Cyrus? Have you heard what Yash is doing?"

He looked blank. "Doing? Is that him making that boom-boom noise?"

"Far worse, Cyrus!" she said, her eyes filling with tears. "It's the moon, that God thing! You said something was going to happen."

He sat her down and held her hand. "Easy, Miouda, my dearest! Start at the beginning and tell me what's going on. Then I'll tell you what I've just seen."

She wiped her face on her sleeve. "I'm sorry. I've got that feeling again – you know, that nothing's going to last. I'm afraid the end's very near."

"Nonsense! Come on, tell me. Please."

Yash had made an announcement, she said. To celebrate the safe return of his copemate, Alba was going to stage what he called a 'festival' the day after tomorrow, when the moon was full. It would be the best evening the Albans had ever had. He had cancelled all patrols so everyone could share in the festivities. The streets would be lit with flaming torches, pigs roasted over blazing fires, and a new drink handed round to everyone.

Cyrus groaned. He knew what was coming next.

It was this wine Yash had been making. He had tested it, and found it tasted good and made the drinkers very happy.

"You could say that," interrupted Cyrus wryly. "Very happy

– and very stupid and very ill." He told her about Jannat.

"Poor woman. And when she said she'd 'been with Sakamir', do you think…?"

"Who knows?"

"That sort of relationship, like using the word 'love', is not really approved of in Alba. It's too personal, too individual." She sighed. "Ah, well. And I haven't told you about the noise yet, have I?"

Researching the festivals of ancient Rome, Yash learned that drums as well as wine played an important part. Accordingly, he and a few hand-picked craftsmen had made six drums from wood and animal skins. That was the noise Cyrus had heard – the drummers practising for the festival.

The Emir had ended his proclamation with an announcement, Miouda said. He was going to change his title from 'Emir' to 'King', and Sakamir would become his 'Queen'. During the festival, the new arrangement would be marked with what he called a 'coronation'. It wasn't a very important change, he assured people, and he'd explain everything carefully when the time came.

"Two days," muttered Cyrus. "We have just two days to save Alba, and probably the Soterion as well."

Suggesting Miouda bar the door of the Ghasar after he'd gone, he hurried out to find Bahm.

Bahm lived with his copemate of three years' standing, a tall, loose-limbed woman with a freckled face and long red hair, in the dormitory reserved for Konnels with regular partners. He

191

was asleep when Cyrus arrived. On waking and recognising his visitor, he pulled on a grubby smock and went outside to talk with him.

He was not surprised to see Cyrus, he said. After Yash's announcement, he had been expecting him. He was, in his own words, 'boiling like an angry pot' at what the Emir was doing.

Cyrus was too, he assured him. He limited his remarks to the proposed festival and coronation, and steered clear of what Sakamir had been up to. Bahm understood facts only. As there weren't enough of these to act on, he decided speculation about a link-up with the Zeds would only complicate matters.

Over Yash's crimes, the pair were in full agreement. In cancelling patrols, holding a festival and changing his title to 'king', he was betraying the position of Emir. He was nothing short of a traitor, Bahm declared, just as Padmar had been.

"Right," said Cyrus. "I agree. But we've got no more than a couple of days. Any suggestions?"

Bahm rubbed a fist thoughtfully through his beard. "Well, you and me hasn't always been friends, Cyrus. Ever since you showed up, even afore that, there's been trouble. Not your fault, maybe, but trouble all the same. Since I'm all for a quiet and peaceful life, here's what I propose.

"I don't think we can stop this daft festival thing – people are too excited about it. That means Yash will go ahead and make himself a king. But that'll help us. When he's up there, being all kingy and mighty, everyone'll see how wrong it is. The archers respect us, Cyrus. Most will come over to our side when we explain what we're doing, like they followed Yash

192

when he turned against Padmar and Timur.

"We'll get rid of Yash and that woman of his, and return to the good old days." He turned to Cyrus with a triumphant grin. "And to make it happen, you know what you've got to do, don't you?"

Cyrus felt a numbness steal over his heart. "I can guess."

"Good. You put all that Soterion stuff back in the cave where it came from, lock the door and throw away the key. Then all will be well again."

Cyrus clenched his fists in frustration. To save the Soterion, they had to destroy Yash; but destroying Yash meant sacrificing the Soterion. It was an impossible position.

"Well, Cyrus, do we have a bargain?"

"For goodness sake, Bahm!" he cried. "It's not about bargains. I'm sorry, but you don't know what you're saying! We're in worse danger than you realise. Much, much worse."

10

The Festival

On the night of the coronation, the moon rose like molten metal over the empty land beyond the walls. The grey buildings of Alba gleamed silver in its light. Within the settlement, from fifty balconies and eaves, battlements and stairways, fiery torches hung. Their seething flames, orange and amber-red, flared into the thick warm air. Yash looked out upon all this and was pleased. Silver and gold were royal colours, he had read, a perfect combination for a crowning. And the light would help what was to follow – mischief is not always best carried out in the dark.

With the moonlight came the drumming. The six performers clambered onto a wooden platform at the top of the square, grinned at each other, and began. New to their art, they started with a steady unison throb – boom, boom, boom, boom – that broadcast their sober heartbeat to the world. Later, as the festival grew in intensity, their rhythms grew faster and bolder.

Drum spoke to drum, each arousing the other to greater frenzy. The players, swept up in the joy of their new-found skill, forgot themselves and the occasion in the swelling pulse of intoxicating sound.

And with the moonlight and the drumming came the wine, thick and bitter and warm. Trusted archers from Yash's patrol carried it down from the terraces in buckets that they placed beside the well for all to help themselves. At first only the bold dipped their cups into the red liquor. The taste was sharp and strange, they said. Perhaps a little disappointing… But not for long. They were soon laughing, staggering a little, and pressing the fermentation on their friends. It's good, they said. Very good. Men, women, children – there was scarce an Alban without the tell-tale red stain about their lips. As inhibitions slid away, normally cautious Constants fell into animated conversation while behind them couples fumbled and sighed in the flickering shadows.

Now the meat was ready. Ten of the finest carcasses, Yash had decreed, prepared in ten different places around the settlement. Each animal was turned over fire until the pork was a crisp and succulent brown, and rich fat dripped, spurting into the embers below. The Konnels, except for Bahm and a fellow dissident, carved generous slices and handed them to the grinning people. Standing in line to receive their bounty, they'd never before experienced anything as good as this. It was so new, so exciting, so all-embracing. Such was the festival's allure, hardly one of them spared a thought for the morrow.

Yash's education had been slow but methodical. Page by

careful page, he had laboriously worked his way through stories of Roman ritual, learning how kings and emperors had secured their power by pleasing the masses. 'Bread and circuses', he read; he wasn't sure what circuses were, but he grasped the theory. People were happier with full stomachs – so he had fed them. They liked ritual – so he had given them one. The mob could be manipulated in a way impossible with individuals, so he would bend and twist the Albans to his will. And when he had finished, there could be no going back.

The Emir kept himself and his copemate out of sight while the festival got under way. Now that everyone had eaten their fill and their minds were loosened by wine, he made his appearance. Emerging out of the shadows behind the drums, he walked to the front of the platform.

"Friends, citizens of Alba," he began, speaking slowly so his voice carried over the carpet of glowing, upturned faces that covered the square. "Listen!" When the last murmur had died away and the throng stood still and expectant, he continued. "This night is very special!"

"Yeah!" cried a voice. A wave of laughter swept through the crowd, followed by spontaneous clapping. Again, Yash raised his hands and the noise gradually died down.

"A special night because we have a festival." Knowing the remark would provoke a response, he added, "Do you like our festival?"

As he had predicted, the tipsy mob howled its response. "Yes! Yes! Yes!"

Yash smiled with inward satisfaction. It was better than he

had expected, much better – Alba was at his feet, adoring him. At this moment, the people would give him whatever he wanted. And then, at the time of his triumph, an unsettling thought came to him. Did he need the Zeds any more? He could take control of Alba and the Soterion without them. He felt the presence of his clever, cold copemate behind him. The dangerous alliance with the barbarians had been her idea – the only certain way of securing the Soterion, she said. Tonight's events had proved her wrong.

The realisation brought him no comfort. Sweat broke out on his forehead and he swept an uneasy hand through his hair. Questions tumbled through his mind, tripping over each other in their haste. Was there a way of calling off the Zed attack? If he warned them now, at this late stage, were the Albans in a fit state to resist? Sakamir's plan was for the Zeds to destroy all Alban opposition – had she really managed to get them to agree to that? Had she told him all she knew? In fact, could he trust her at all?

The cheers had subsided and the crowd was expecting him to tell them what came next. With a final sweep of his hair, he forced himself back to the present. It was too late for a change of plan. The only way was forward – forward to power, to control of the Soterion, to the Salvation Project and victory over death itself.

"This festival is not for me – it is for the heart and spirit of Alba – it is for you!" he exclaimed, building to a climax on the final phrase. Further cheers. "Because I – your chosen leader – care for you."

"Yash! Yash! Yash!" rose the chant. He let it run for a while before continuing. "And because I care for you, because recently we saw what happens when a leader does not care, I will surrender the title of Emir." The crowd groaned. "Don't worry! I won't abandon you. Instead of your Emir, I will be your king!

"The Long Dead had kings. Kings were fathers of their people, caring for them, guiding them, protecting them. So will I look after you." He paused and looked round the crowd. "Fellow Albans, my friends, tell me: Is this ... is this really ... is this really what you want? Speak to me!"

The roar of approval carried high into the night sky. It rolled through the streets, up the terraces, over the walls and into the wasteland beyond. There, hidden in the trees, Malika Xsani heard it and turned to her kumfort. "Good, Jintha. It ith jutht ath Thakamir thaid it would be."

Back in Alba, Sakamir handed Yash a woven circlet of vines. "This," he cried, holding it up for all to see, "is a crown! It is worn by kings to show their majesty. Look!"

He raised the garland over his head and slowly brought it down until it rested around his brow. "I am now crowned," he explained. "At this moment, in Long Dead times, the crowd shouted, 'Long live the king!'"

He needed to say no more. "Long live the king!" howled the crowd. "Long live the king! Long live the king!"

How appropriate, thought Yash. When I have the Salvation Project, I'll certainly live a long, long time. He took Sakamir by the hand and led her forward. "Every king has a queen," he announced. Lifting the crown from his own head, he placed it on Sakamir's. "There! You have a king and a queen, just like the Long Dead."

The crowd's yelling was less raucous this time. Sensing it was time to bring the ceremony to a close, he shouted, "Albans, my subjects, the coronation is over! Thank you for your support. I – we – will not let you down. On with the festival! More drums! More wine! The best is still to come!"

As the cheers echoed about him, the new king led his queen off the platform and across the square to the Emiron. So thrilled was he by his triumph, he failed to notice that she was still wearing the crown.

As Yash and Sakamir left the platform, the drummers struck up once more. The beat was faster, more insistent, and for the first time in their lives, the Albans began to dance. Swaying, stamping, waving, reeling and clapping, they allowed their bodies to move instinctively to the rhythm of the night. Around the well, beakers splashed into the wine buckets, filling and refilling. Things were said that should never have been said; things were done that should never have been done. In one short evening, the culture that had held Alba together for generations fell apart. Like a soldier who has set aside his armour, the community lay open and vulnerable to the enemy.

Cyrus, as experienced a warrior as anyone in Alba, knew this. At the beginning of the evening, soon after the drumming had begun, he had climbed to the lower terrace with Miouda and Sammy. Corby, ever the loyal and patient companion, lay panting at his master's feet. Seated on the low stone wall, the three friends gazed at the extraordinary events unfolding below. Cyrus, despite his misgivings, marvelled at the vivid richness of the scene: the cold moonlight and the fiery flames of the torches and cooking fires, the mouth-watering smell of roasting pork, the snatches of distant conversation, cries and laughter, and over it all the bewitching rhythm of the drums.

"You want to go down?" he asked Miouda. "They're enjoying themselves."

She shook her head. "No thanks, Cyrus. I'm happy just watching."

He smiled. "What about you, Sammy?"

The young man put his head on one side. "Mmm … maybe. Sounds fun, doesn't it? Yeah, I think I'll go and take a quick look for myself at what's going on." With that, he was off down the slope with Corby bounding beside him.

"Don't stay too long!" Cyrus called after him. "Remember what it's all about!" The caution drowned in the sound of the drums long before it reached him.

After he'd been gone a while, Cyrus noticed a group of figures advancing along the terrace. He stood up, peering into the darkness. "Thought I might be finding you here," said a gruff voice. "Going mad down there, aren't they?"

It was Bahm. He, his freckle-faced copemate and seven of their friends – four men and three women – had taken one look at what was going on and left in disgust. It made him want to weep, he said.

"Me too," said Cyrus, inviting the new arrivals to sit beside them. They talked about the change in Yash, about Sakamir's return, and about the purpose of the festival.

"I don't mind them drum things," said Bahm, tapping the rhythm on his knee. "But I don't like that wine stuff. What's it supposed to do, send you to sleep?"

"No, at least not straight away," said Cyrus. "It's got something in it called alcohol that changes the way your brain works…" He broke off and sprang to his feet. "Oh no! Where's Sammy? He went ages ago." Without another word, he sprinted off towards the square.

"Sammy! Sammy!" he called as he pushed through the throng gathering before the platform. "Sammy? Anyone seen Sammy?"

He finally caught sight of him, flush-faced, leaning against a wall talking to a pair of young women. They were all laughing. As Cyrus watched, one of the women stooped and patted Corby on the head. Sammy was gesturing wildly with his left hand. In the other he held a beaker.

"Sammy!" Cyrus called. Anger and sorrow welled within him. He dodged round an archer who had his arm round the waist of a heavily pregnant woman, and ran up to his friend.

"What the…?" he cried, dashing the beaker from Sammy's hand so it smashed to pieces at his feet. "I told you … Jannat … I warned you! Can't you see what's going on? It's a trap!"

Sammy looked at him blankly. "If's trap, is very nice one!" he slurred.

Cyrus grabbed him by the collar. "Sorry, Sammy, but you're coming with me!"

"Oi, Cyrus!" shouted the shorter of the two women. "Leave

him alone! He's having fun!"

"Maybe fun now," snapped Cyrus. "But you wait…"

Half dragging him, half lifting him, he hauled Sammy over to the well and pushed his head into the water bucket. "Drink!" he commanded. Beside him, Corby sniffed at the red liquid in an abandoned cup and wondered whether it was this that had made his master behave so strangely. He licked cautiously at the surface.

The crowd around them laughed. Cyrus should stick Sammy's head into a wine bucket, they joked, just like the dog was doing. He ignored their banter and, as Yash was beginning his speech, he elbowed his way to the edge of the crowd and led his friend stumbling back up the terrace. For the first time in his life, Corby did not follow his master.

"I'm sorry," Cyrus said as he lowered Sammy onto the wall beside Miouda, "but we need your help. If you'd stayed down there, we might never have seen you or Corby again."

At the time, he did not realise how close to the mark his words were.

During Yash and Sakamir's coronation, Cyrus explained as best he could what was going on. He knew much less than Yash on the subject, though he had read enough to see that the Albans were being hoodwinked. As far as he could remember, the Long Dead had done away with kings and emperors – some good, some bad – a long time before the Great Death. That was why, he imagined, Constant settlements had been established with rules that allowed the people to choose their own leaders. Yash was not taking Alba back to 2017 but to a time long before that. He had to be stopped.

As he was speaking, they became aware of someone else making their way up the slope in their direction. It was Jannat. She had been looking for Cyrus everywhere, she said. She wanted to apologise. She couldn't remember exactly what she had said or done after Yash's wine testing, but she was deeply ashamed. While searching for Cyrus, she had tried to warn others about the effects of the wine but few were prepared to listen. She was being a killjoy, she was told, trying to stop others doing what she herself had done a couple of days previously.

Cyrus welcomed her. He'd forgotten their meeting by the well, he said – there were far more important things to worry about. As briefly as he could, he outlined the fears shared by Bahm, himself and the others in the group. Their mission, very simply, was to save Alba. Jannat, her face pale and serious, pledged herself to the cause.

But what cause? Bahm asked. It wasn't quite as straight-forward as Cyrus made out. Both men agreed that Yash was destroying the settlement. But while Cyrus blamed the man himself, Bahm said the Soterion was the real root of the problem. Its influence was doing more harm than good. He admitted that after Jalus' cure he had thought it might be worth preserving. But seeing what Yash was doing, he had reverted to his old position. He did not want to burn the books; he just wanted them restored to the vault and the key destroyed. Then everything could return to normal.

"Even if I agreed with you, which you know I don't," replied Cyrus, "it's probably already too late to put the books back."

"How so?"

Looking around to check that they were not overheard, Cyrus signalled for the others to gather closely round him. What he had to say was of deadly importance. If it was true, then they had to act at once, not wait for the morning.

"It's about Sakamir," he said. "I'm not sure, but I think, while she was away, she may have come to an agreement with the Zeds."

"Eh?" said Bahm, frowning deeply. "Agreement to do what?"

Against the noise of the frenzied festival, Cyrus outlined his theory. He explained about Timur's head, about Sakamir's willingness to go out into Zed territory, about how she had behaved after her escape compared with Roxanne, about the lure of the Soterion and the Salvation Project, and about why Yash had done his best to lower Alba's defences. There was an ominous silence when he finished, followed by an avalanche of questions.

Everyone except Sammy wanted to know more. The dousing with cold water and the experience of being dragged up the hillside had quickly sobered him up, and he tried to focus on what was being said. It was impossible – he was plagued by guilt. In a few stupid moments, he had failed his two best friends. He had made a fool of himself in front of Cyrus and allowed Corby to go missing. The dog would find his way back, of that he was sure. He remembered going down to the square with him and he half-remembered seeing him when Cyrus was shoving his head in a bucket. Yes, Corby would be alright.

But Cyrus? How could he begin to make it up to the man who was everything to him – rescuer, friend, hero, guardian and role model? Since escaping from the Children of Gova and joining the Soterion Mission, he had done his best to live up to his father figure's expectations. Despite blindness in one eye, he had made himself into a half-decent archer, learned to read quicker than most, discovered heaps of things about the ways of the Long Dead… And this evening he had spoiled it all.

Cyrus had been cross with him only once before, when he challenged him to cure Jalus. But he had never seen him as angry as he had been in the square. Worse, he had been upset, too – and it was Sammy's own fault! And he would have done it at this crucial moment, when the fate of their mission was in the balance, wouldn't he? What a thick-headed idiot he'd been! Forcing himself to concentrate, he listened to the talk a while longer. As he did so, it dawned on him what he had to do to make things right again. Of course! He checked his knife and, without a word to the others, slipped quietly off into the night.

"Well, how about that?" said Yash, shutting the front door of the Emiron behind him. "I deserve a little reward, don't I, Sakamir?"

He walked up behind her and slid his arms round her waist. "What do you think the king and queen should do now, eh?" he asked, pulling her closer.

For a moment, Sakamir froze. She then carefully unclasped his hands and turned to face him. "Later, Your Majesty. We have things to sort out first, don't we?"

Yash exhaled noisily in frustration. "As usual! Oh well, if you insist. But afterwards we'll enjoy ourselves, ok?"

She flashed him one of her blank smiles. "Yes, afterwards

I'll certainly enjoy myself a lot. And I hope you will too, dear copemate."

"Ha! Can't wait!"

"You'll have to. But not for long, I promise." She took off her crown and threw it casually into a corner. "Right, to business. I'm not quite sure, King Yash, that we're sticking to our original plan, are we?"

He sat on the floor and lay back against a hay-filled cushion. "To be honest, Sakamir, things have changed a bit. I'm more powerful now, so I'm not sure we still need those Zeds of yours."

"Oh?"

"You see, I've got such tight control over the place they'll do whatever I want. I'm sure there are enough good readers who'll support me. I know you don't agree, but I say it's time to get rid of Cyrus and that woman of his, and take over the Soterion for ourselves. Then we'll find the Salvation Project, using that electricity stuff if necessary – and there we are. All done without a single Zed."

Throughout this speech, Sakamir stood looking down at the man lounging at her feet. What contempt she had for him! He was just a great child – a cunning one, perhaps, but still a child. And stupid. He was making things difficult for her. Fool! He was forcing her into a change of plan. So be it. What she had arranged for the Grozny to do, she would now have to do herself. It was something she had been wanting to do for a long time, anyway. But she had to be very careful. At this stage of the operation, there was no room for error...

"You make it sound so easy," she said, loosening her gown

and lying languidly beside him. "But you are ignoring one or two important things, aren't you, Yash? First, as I told you when you imprisoned him, we still need Cyrus. He can't be trusted, of course, but there are Zeds who understand exactly how to tame a man."

Yash frowned. "Listening to you, Sakamir, one might think you actually liked those Zeds. They are barbarians, you know!"

"Of course! And we're not. Anyway, my second point: tomorrow, the effects of your wine will have worn off. As we found when we tested it, it does not leave people in a good mood."

"That's their fault. They'll still listen to me."

"Or to Bahm? Or Cyrus?"

"Eh?"

"Your Majesty was so wrapped up in his speech, he didn't look carefully at the crowd, did he? I did. I saw who was and who was not there."

"Meaning?"

"A handful of people stayed away from the square. Not many, but they were important. People like Cyrus and Bahm and two other Konnels. They're probably plotting against you even now, Yash. So you do need my Zeds, don't you?"

"I doubt it. Still think it's best to call them off. All we have to do is keep the gates shut. Even drunk guards will be able to keep them out."

That sealed it. Time for her to move. With a sigh of resignation, she raised herself onto one elbow and kissed Yash full on the mouth. "Ah well! I said 'later', didn't I?" she whispered huskily.

"Do you think this is late enough?"

"Mmm!" He stretched out a strong arm and pulled her on top of him.

"Ow!" She rolled quickly away.

"What is is it?"

"Your knife, Yash. It was sticking into me. Here, let me take your belt off. That's better. Your knife's very sharp, isn't it? It could cause a nasty accident…"

From the terrace Sammy made his way to a point some hundred paces above the square and sat for a moment searching for Corby. No sign. Ah well! he sighed. The dog was quite capable of looking after himself – and his master had something very important to do.

Yash was behind everything that was going wrong, wasn't he? He'd lowered Alba's guard and persuaded the people to make him king so he could do what he wanted. If he wasn't around, there wouldn't be a problem. Cyrus and Bahm could warn about a possible Zed attack and get the guards back on the walls. They could deal with everything if Yash wasn't around… If Yash wasn't around…

Sammy had killed only once, when he had finished off the Zed pinned to the ground by Corby during the Grozny attack. If he could do it once, he told himself as he skirted round the edge of the square on his way to the Emiron, he could do it again. He eased his knife in its scabbard, making sure he could draw it freely. There was no point charging in, he decided – Yash was stronger and a more experienced fighter. He had to rely on surprise, strike at close range.

The Emiron was on the right side of a cul-de-sac at the north-east corner of Lion Square. A brick building with a roof of crude thatch, it had once been a store house. Several years previously, an Emir had made it her personal residence and her successors had kept the tradition going. Sammy knew the place. He had called in shortly after arriving in Alba, so although from the outside it was like the other store houses in the area, he had no difficulty identifying it.

He had made a quick plan on his way down from the terrace. Yash must be destroyed, that was certain. If necessary, he'd sacrifice his own life in the process. But he was no saint. He wasn't looking for martyrdom and saw no point in taking deliberate risks. So rather than carry on through the square, even though he might find Corby there, he skirted round to the left. Reaching the piles of rubble and other rubbish at the end of the street where the Emiron stood, he flattened himself against the wall of the next-door building.

Now what? Yash might have gone out to show himself to his people again. In that case, Sammy would wait for him to return before striking. He hoped Cyrus wouldn't come looking for him in the meantime. And what if Sakamir was also at home? He'd have to kill her too. That would be tricky. Realising this sort of thinking undermined his determination, he clenched his fists and told himself to get on with it. He'd deal with problems as they arose.

He drew his dagger and peered cautiously into the street. The way was clear. He was on the point of stepping out when he heard Yash's door opening. Someone was coming! He darted back and squatted down in the shadows. Moments later, a figure hurried by, heading away from the square. It was Sakamir. He watched carefully as she edged round the rubbish heaps and disappeared down the slope in the direction of the Soterion Gate.

How strange, he thought. But at least he wouldn't have to deal with two of them. He slipped out of his hiding place and, keeping in the shadow at the side of the street, edged his way to the door of the Emiron.

Knock or burst straight in? Not wanting to alarm Yash, he tapped lightly on the door. No reply. He knocked again, harder this time. Still no reply.

Gingerly, Sammy put his hand on the latch and pushed the door open. Not a sound. He paused on the threshold and called quietly, "Yash? Hello!" Receiving no response, he called again. "Hello? Are you there, Yash?" Not a whisper.

He hid his dagger behind his back, went inside and shut the door quietly behind him. The single large room was lit by one of the new oil lamps. Sammy looked around. Ah! Yash had not gone out. Head thrown back and arms and legs outstretched, the self-appointed king lay sprawled across a large cushion. He was fast asleep.

At least I won't have to fight, Sammy told himself. His hand shook as he brought out his knife. Standing there, summoning up the courage to strike, he wished Corby were with him. He missed the animal's wet nose nuzzling against his leg at moments like this. He wanted to reach down and give his long ears a reassuring tickle. The thought made him pause, awe-struck at what he was about to do. No, he reminded himself, this is not murder. This is execution. I'm just doing what the archers did to Padmar. It's what all traitors deserve.

Fixing his eyes on his quarry, he advanced cautiously. Quite what happened next, he wasn't sure. Either because of his partial blindness or because he was concentrating so hard on Yash, he didn't notice the floor directly beneath him. Half way between the door and the sleeping figure, he stepped in something dark and slippery. His left leg shot from under him and he crashed headlong forward. Instinctively, he put out his left hand to break his fall. It hit Yash on the shoulder, rolling him off the cushion and onto the floor. There he lay, motionless.

Almost sick with fear, Sammy scrambled to his feet and picked up the lamp from the low table to his right. He was shaking so much it took him a while to get the light where he wanted it. When he did so, he gasped in astonishment.

The sticky substance he had slipped on was blood. Yash's blood. Sammy followed the warm, purple-black stream along the floor to its bleeding source. The King of Alba's throat had not simply been cut, it had been hacked wide open. The gash, deep and wide, ran right across his neck from cheek to pallid cheek. In the half-light, it looked like a freshly cut slice of watermelon.

Quivering and open-mouthed, Sammy stared in amazement. He had seen countless dead bodies before, including some cruelly slain in warfare. But this was different. Whoever had murdered Yash – and he was pretty sure who it was – had done so with a mechanical, cynical viciousness. They had wanted not simply to kill, but to butcher him. It was an act of passionate hatred.

A shout from the crowd in the square brought him to his senses. How ironic, he thought, to be found with the corpse of the man he had come to execute, but who had actually been slain by another. No one would believe his innocence. He had to get out, fast.

He crossed to the door, grasped the handle – and stopped. *No, wait. I'll never get this chance again – I can't just walk out empty-handed.* Letting go of the handle, he returned to the centre of the room.

"It must be here somewhere," he muttered to himself. "Must be."

Urgently, trying not to get too much blood on his own clothing, he searched Yash's body. Nothing. Holding the lamp high, he scoured the walls and the heap of bedding at the far end of the room. Nothing there either. He went through the assorted mugs, beakers, plates and storage jars piled on shelves along the back wall. Still nothing. Maybe Sakamir had taken it? That really would make things difficult.

Another drunken yell from the square made him jump. He must leave. Turning towards the door, he gave a final glance round the room. The shelves, the body, the cushion... The cushion?

One cut sliced open the bag, allowing its dusty contents to tumble to the floor. Hay, just hay. No, wait. What was that? Yes!

"Double success!" he whispered as he stooped and picked

up the object he had been looking for. Putting it into the pouch on his belt, he hurried out into the street without even bothering to close the door behind him.

11

Revenge of the Zeds

"I couldn't believe it, Cyrus," said Sammy, still panting after his run up to the lower terrace. "Never knew one person had so much blood in him."

"And you're sure it was Sakamir?" asked Cyrus.

Sammy glanced at the men and women gathered around him. "Had to be. I mean, I saw her come out, and when I went in he was still bleeding."

"Not surprised," muttered Bahm. "She always were vicious."

"Sort of glad, in a way," Sammy said quietly. "Means I didn't have to do it. But I would have," he went on, louder. "I really would. I wanted to save everything we've been doing; you know, the mission, the Soterion, the books and all that. Trying to make a better world for everyone. Now she's done it for us." He paused and looked around anxiously. "Corby come back yet?"

Cyrus shook his head. "Sorry, no sign of him, Sammy." The young man's face fell. "And I don't want to make things worse, but I don't think you're right about what Sakamir's done."

"How come?"

"I don't think her killing Yash will make a better world for everyone."

"More likely an even worse one," cut in Miouda. "She was thinking of just one person – herself. It ties in with what we've been saying. You reckon she was heading for the gate, Sammy?"

"Yeah. Why?"

Cyrus jumped to his feet. "Because I have a horrible feeling she's going to let her friends in."

Bahm rose to stand beside him. "Friends? You mean Zeds?"

"Precisely," said Cyrus. "There are no guards on duty, almost the whole population is drunk, the Emir is dead – can you think of a better time to try to take over this place?"

"So we've got to stop her, haven't we?" cried Sammy.

"Right. Grab whatever weapon you can find," yelled Cyrus, "and do as I say. I'll go down to the Soterion Gate with Miouda, Jannat and Sammy. Bahm, you and your copemate run to the patrol gate. If it's already open, do whatever it takes to shut it again. The rest of you spread out and warn people about what's going on.

"If we hurry, we can still save the place. Let's go!"

After Sakamir's departure, Xsani had worked hard to build up a sense of trust between the three tribes under her command. The last thing she wanted was a civil war on the way to Alba or within its walls. Getting groups of Zeds to work together was never easy, and the task was all the harder when one of them was female. The key, as she had realised at the beginning of her campaign, was Timur.

Ogg was no problem. Half-blind and terrified of castration, he continued to accept Xsani's leadership – delivered through Timur – without dissent. Periodic visits to the sty topped up his loyalty to the legendary Over-Malik. By and large, the Gurkov did as he said – those who did not were brutally punished. To reinforce his command, Xsani organised a repeat Timur adoration ceremony in Filna's central piazza.

"Timur! Timur! Timur!" roared the Gurkov, waving their fists and gazing in rapture at the blackened totem suspended before them.

The Grozny received a similar reminder of their Over-Malik's majesty, and they too mindlessly chanted his name before the skull. But Xsani still found their leader something of an enigma. Giv had learned all that Teach, his Constant slave, had to offer. He could count, speak fluently and understood abstract concepts like 'power' and 'ambition'. So sharp had he become that the Malika sometimes had to remind herself that he was merely a dumbman Zed.

What really mystified her were his continued obsessions. Every dumbman she had ever met had wanted only one thing from her – but not Giv. He seemed happy to stare at her, wide-eyed and open-mouthed. Just a fleeting touch from her hand sent him into paroxysms of delight. It was so strange!

Giv's relationship with the Over-Malik was even more weird. She couldn't believe he still took the totem seriously, but he did. He adored that thing, that shrunken clump of bone, skin and hair. Nor was he acting when he spoke with Timur's voice – to him it was Timur's voice and he was simply a mouthpiece. It was ridiculous! Dead people didn't speak.

The idea of Timur talking was as stupid as the Long Dead picture in her residence showing crowds of people gazing at the dead dumbman in the large yellow hat. It was pointless. The dead were gone, finished. That was what her plan to get the Soterion was all about, wasn't it? Once its knowledge was hers, she would force dumbman Cyrus to find the Salvation Project. With that, she would defeat death. Her power would be limitless and eternal. No more would fools adore shrunken heads or dead dumbmen in yellow hats – everyone, the whole world, would adore her!

Malika Xsani would reign supreme.

Two days before the full moon, Xsani gave the order to march. Her forces went in three columns. The Kogon were in the centre, led by Timur's head carried high on a spike; the Grozny took the left flank and the Gurkov the right. To check that Sakamir had not been luring them into an ambush, Kogon Eyes scoured the countryside ahead of them as they advanced.

By the time they reached the woods that surrounded Alba, they had met not a soul. Xsani was relieved. Though no traitor could ever be really trusted, Sakamir had told the truth when she said patrols had been cancelled. Would she now open Alba's gates to them?

Early in the evening of the festival, Xsani divided her forces. The Gurkov were lined up opposite the Soterion Gate. Giv's

Grozny were sent higher up the mountain, where the defensive wall was lower. Xsani concealed the Kogon in trees facing the Patrol Gate. It was a deliberate choice: once inside, they would be only a short distance from the Ghasar. As the moon rose behind them, all was ready for the assault. Everything depended on Sakamir.

Yash's murder had been a messy business. The blood came out in spurts, splashing over her face and hair and down the front of her tunic in a most disagreeable manner. She managed to wipe some of it off. Nevertheless, Alba's new queen was a pretty gruesome sight and was relieved to reach the Soterion Gate without meeting anyone. Remaining in the shadows, she glanced around. Not a guard to be seen. She heaved at the heavy wooden bar that held the gates shut. After a brief struggle, she raised one end from its iron bracket and, using it as a lever, pulled the gate open.

From the darkness outside a raucous cheer arose, followed by the sound of feet running towards the gate. Sakamir darted up the steps that led to the battlements. Despite her Z tattoo, she had no intention of being in the way when the Gurkov came howling into Alba intent on slaughter, rape and pillage. Zeds were not renowned for their discrimination.

At the top of the steps, she paused. Below and to her left, a stream of barbarian warriors was making for the opening. A number had already passed through and she could hear the first screams of dismay as they fell upon the unsuspecting Albans. Beyond them, in the square, the revellers danced on.

Sakamir glanced along the wall towards the Patrol Gate. She had to get there soon, open it to let in the Kogon and dash up to the Ghasar. She had to reach it before the Zeds. Once in possession, the final stage of her plan could begin.

By morning, Cyrus and one or two others from his class would be the only Albans left alive. After Xsani had 'tamed' them, Sakamir would kill her. She hadn't decided how, but something along the lines of the Yash murder probably. She'd put the blame on Jinsha. No, not her – on Yalisha. She wanted Jinsha for herself. The stupid smoked head would come next. Once she had that in her possession, the Kogon, Grozny and Gurkov would fall in behind her. At that point – commanding three tribes, in control of the Soterion and the only people able to read – her triumph would be complete.

Like so many dreams, it was as simple as it was impossible.

As she ran in the direction of the Patrol Gate, Sakamir saw three figures clambering unsteadily up a wooden ladder to the battlements. At the top, they would be directly between her and her destination. She couldn't avoid them. Fortunately for her, they weren't there for any military purpose – full of wine and oppressed by the stifling atmosphere in the square, they were looking for a breath of fresh air. None of them was armed.

Without breaking her pace, Sakamir crashed straight into the astonished revellers. Her knife pierced the first in the stomach; the second she pushed off the wall onto the rocks below; the third, terror-stricken by the bloodstained fiend careering out of the darkness, fled towards the ladder. Sakamir's knife plunged directly between her shoulder blades.

On reaching the gate, she sped down the wooden steps and threw back the bolts fastening the door. A sharp hiss told her the Kogon were on their way. Immediately, she turned and ran towards the Ghasar. By the fireburn rock, she passed Bahm and his copemate running hard in the opposite direction. Moments later, she heard a ferocious roar as he launched himself on the intruders. Bloodcurdling shouts and clashes ended in a long hiss of triumph.

Sakamir, half-expecting to meet Cyrus in the Ghasar, was relieved to find it empty. A pair of oil lamps threw flickering shadows onto the walls and ceiling. Closing the door, she arranged the lamps on either side of her and sat on a stack of books placed against the back wall. There, seated on a throne of learning, the Queen of Alba listened to the sounds of her handiwork.

The drumming had stopped. In its place a hideous cacophony of screams and yells floated up from the square. The queen smiled with satisfaction. The massacre of her people was going well, she noted. Everything was falling into place just as she had planned.

She had to wait longer than she expected for Xsani to appear. And when the Malika finally pushed open the door and looked cautiously round, Sakamir had the strange sensation of waking from a dream.

The normal route from the lower terrace to the Soterion Gate passed through Lion Square. Cyrus glanced down at the seething crowd.

"We'll never get through that lot," he decided. "Better along the wall. Come on!"

Followed by Miouda, Jannat and Sammy, he sprinted left along the terrace. At its end, they crossed the path and an area of scrub to the wall. In this section, the concrete inward face was low enough for Cyrus to leap straight onto the battlement. He pulled the others up after him and they ran along the top towards the gate.

As their destination came into sight, they saw at once they were too late. Although the moon was on the wane, there was sufficient light to make out a dark surge of figures pouring into the settlement. The quicker runners had already reached the square and begun massacring the terrified Albans.

Cyrus turned away in despair. Jannat gasped and covered her face with her hands. Sammy reached down instinctively to stroke Corby and, finding him not there, stared in open-mouthed disbelief at the dreadful scene. He knew he would probably never see his dog again.

Miouda was the first to speak. "Oh, Alba!" she wept. "What have we done to deserve this? All our friends ... all our work ... all we believed in..."

She stood in silence for a moment, taking in the full horror of what was happening. Then, with an extraordinary effort of will and showing a side of her the others had rarely seen, she said, "But we can't give up, we just can't. This is Sakamir's doing, so she can seize the Soterion. But we can still stop her."

Cyrus read her mind. "Yes – as long as we get to the Ghasar before her. It's pretty extreme, but it's our only chance."

"But worth trying," continued Miouda. "We'll grab the SP laptop – and another two or three if we can manage it – then set fire to the place."

"What?" cried Sammy. "Burn all them books?"

"Yes. She'll be left with nothing – but we'll have whatever's in the laptops. If we can get out of here with them, find a source of electricity –"

"If, if, if…" cut in Sammy. "Too many ifs, Miouda."

"There isn't any other way, Sammy," said Cyrus. "Burning the books will break my heart – and we don't even know whether the laptops work – but what else? And we've got no time, so let's do it."

He clenched his fists in determination. "We'll return to the terraces – we should be safe there for a while. I'll dash down to the Ghasar, grab a couple of laptops and bring them back to base. After that, we'll figure out a way of getting out of here."

Miouda shook her head. "No, Cyrus. You're not going alone –"

"Yes, Miouda! It's my duty. No argument – and there's no point in risking life unnecessarily. Besides, it'll be easier on my own. Less conspicuous."

She gave him a look that seemed to say she agreed but wanted to add something else. In the end, she kept quiet and the four friends turned to run back along the wall.

Miouda's plan almost failed before it began. They had hardly taken a step before seven or eight pairs of grimy, broken-nailed hands appeared on the edge of the parapet. A shaggy head emerged … and another.

They were Grozny. Giv's orders were to lead his men over

the mountain wall, sweep across the terraces and cut off a possible escape route from that direction. The strategy was good, his execution of it less so. Though Alba's wall was low in this sector, it stood at the top of a jagged rockface. Charging at it mindlessly, several Grozny fell off before reaching the top. Those who made it to the foot of the wall stared blankly up at the concrete scarp, clueless how to surmount it. Only after Giv had shouted up to them to help each other – behaviour alien to their Zed nature – did they try lifting one another up to the battlement. These were the figures confronting the Constants trying to return to the terraces.

Well-aimed kicks sent half a dozen Grozny spinning down to the ground. But still the barbarians came on. Eventually three made it to the top of the wall ahead of the Constants, blocking their path. With more Zeds making it to the parapet behind them, retreat was impossible. Nor could they get away by jumping down on the inward side – at this point the wall rose sheer to a height of three people. They were trapped.

The Constants' knives were no match for the spear and gut-rippers wielded by the Zed trio ahead of them. Their only hope was to use the narrowness of the path. Jannat must have sensed this. Pushing past Cyrus, she ran with long, powerful strides straight at the nearest enemy. It was a sacrifice of the noblest Constant kind – she laid down her life for her friends.

The spear of the leading Zed pierced her heart before she reached him. But she was moving with such force that she drove him back onto the man behind, knocking his weapon to one side. Cyrus was onto him in a flash. While his right hand sent the spear-carrier tumbling off the wall, with his left he snatched the gut-ripper off the next man.

It was now no contest. With a single blow of his new weapon, Cyrus felled the warrior he had taken it from. Taking careful aim, he then hurled it at the one remaining Zed. The spike caught the man square in the chest, killing him instantly.

The path was clear. Stepping over the bodies of the fallen, the three Constants ran along the wall to the point where they had first joined it. The Grozny, eager to join the slaughter in the square, didn't bother to give chase.

When they reached a point where the inward face of the wall was no taller than a man, Cyrus and Sammy leaped easily down. Miouda remained on the parapet, strangely reluctant to jump.

"Come on!" yelled Cyrus. "Hurry! Jump!"

She shook her head. "Sorry, Cyrus. You'll have to help me."

Mystified and slightly irritated, he ran up to the wall and raised his arms. Miouda leaned forward, put her hands in his and let him lower her to the ground.

"What was all that about?"

"I'll explain later." She gave him a hurried kiss. "Off you go! We'll be waiting for you on the third terrace. Take great care and whatever you do, Cyrus, come back…"

He was gone before she finished, sprinting across the slope to their right and skirting the square before dipping down towards the children's dormitory above the Ghasar. Miouda and Sammy stood watching until he disappeared from sight. When he had gone, she sat on the edge of the terrace and clasped her hands together in a manner the Long Dead would have called prayer.

"Oh Sammy! I do hope he'll be alright."

"Course he will! I've been in tight scrapes with Cyrus before and he always finds a way out. Tough and clever, he is. Special." He sat beside her and put an arm round her shoulders. "Anyway, we couldn't lose Corby and Cyrus in one evening, could we?"

"Do you think Corby's really gone?"

With tears in his eyes, he nodded towards the square. "Don't reckon anything could live down there. Leastwise, not anything half-decent."

"Oh Sammy! It's so terrible. There's never been anything like it, has there? It's like the end of the world. Listen!"

By moonlight and firelight Grozy and Gurkov, drunk on blood and cruelty, were gorging themselves on acts of unspeakable barbarity, and the hideous sounds of massacre were audible from every corner of the stricken settlement. Miouda was right. It was like the end of the world.

She shivered and looked towards the Patrol Gate. Here, in the sector allocated to the Kogon, the scene was quieter, though no less bloody. She stared hard at the roof of the Ghasar, trying to imagine Cyrus inside, grabbing a laptop and…

"Sammy! Sammy! What's that? Look!"

"Where?"

"By the Ghasar. Smoke!"

As they watched, flames licked upwards from one end of the roof. There was no mistaking it – the Ghasar was on fire! Cyrus had done it!

"Told you he would, didn't I?" said Sammy, giving Miouda a hug.

"Yes. It means a lot to me, Sammy. More than just saving the laptop." He gave her a quizzical look. "Ok, if you promise not to mention it yet, I'll let you into a secret…"

Cyrus had not done it.

The first suggestion of alarm had run through Sakamir the moment Xsani and her bodyguard entered the Ghasar. How stupid she was to have put herself in such a vulnerable position! To gain the Soterion, she had made herself a barbarian: she had accepted the brand of a Zed, murdered Potr and her copemate, and allowed a whole Constant community to be utterly destroyed. It was all justified because now just one human heartbeat stood between her and supreme power.

But as she stared at the Malika – ally and enemy – she knew she had made a dreadful error of judgement. She had assumed that she and Xsani would share control for a few days while Cyrus and other literate Albans were subdued. When the opportunity arose, she would do away with Xsani and…

Do away with Xsani? Yes, there was the rub.

"Tho, here we are," lisped her rival as her bodyguard noiselessly positioned themselves around her. Xsani's blue eyes flicked quickly round the hall, checking for danger. Eventually her gaze came to rest on the queen's bloody dress. "Been butchering?"

Sakamir forced her mouth into a rigid smile. "Yes, it was Yash. As I promised. Welcome to Alba, Malika Xsani. It is ours!"

Arms outstretched, she took a step forward. The bodyguard's spears closed across her path like scissors. She could advance no further.

Her alarm swelled into panic and she found herself trembling like a fevered child. What sort of idiot trusted a Zed? The cool demeanour she had cultivated for so long was cracking up – and she was powerless to stop it. In a moment of paralysing insight, she saw she no longer controlled her own destiny: in destroying Alba, she had destroyed herself.

"Oh, Xsani!" she blurted. "No need for that! We're allies. We have an agreement, remember? I opened the gates for you…" She was pleading, and hated herself for it. It was utterly humiliating – and utterly hopeless.

With the sounds of massacre in her ears, she realised the full and horrible futility of what she had done. She opened her mouth, but no words came. They were spoken in her heart instead. "I'm sorry. Forgive me. Please…"

The confession was interrupted by Xsani, smooth and sweet and deadly. "Oh Thakamir! I am tho dithapointed! I thought you were clever – but no. I thought you were thtrong – but no. And I thought you would be difficult to dethtroy – but no. Farewell."

At a wave of their mistress's hand, four of the bodyguard swung round. Their steel-tipped spears came down as one, levelled at Sakamir's breast.

The Queen of Alba's motives for what she did next will never be known. Had she decided that if she couldn't have the Soterion, no one would? Or was it a desperate attempt to make amends for what she had done, keeping the Soterion out of Zed hands? Whatever prompted her behaviour, the consequences were the same.

Quicker than the spears lunging towards her, Sakamir darted backwards, grabbed the two oil lamps and smashed them together over the stacks of books around her. By the time the spears struck, piercing her to the spine, flaming oil was seeping into the dry papers. There was no water to hand. In vain the bodyguard beat at the fire with their spears before the heat forced them outside. From the books, the flames leaped to the wooden walls and so up to the thatched roof. Soon the whole building was a furious inferno.

The Soterion was no more.

Cyrus saw the blaze as he rounded the children's dormitory. Standing on open ground, oblivious to danger, he stared at the conflagration in horror. The mission, Roxanne's sacrifice, the classes, the hope of a better future ... all gone. Everything had been pointless.

Similar thoughts ran through the mind of Xsani as, standing twenty paces below Cyrus, she gazed at the blazing Ghasar. The creation of the Timur myth, her alliance with those idiotic dumbmans and the surrender of the Kogon's secret identity had all been in vain. She had come so close to seizing the means to supreme power ... she had seen the books, almost touched them ... and now, like her ambition, they were crumbling to ashes.

Overcome with emotions she had never before experienced, she lifted her eyes from the fire to the rising ground behind. There a figure stood, solitary and unmoving. As she looked, he turned his head towards her and their eyes met. She recognised him at once. The commanding physique, firm mouth, eyes wise beyond their time... It had to be him – the only dumbman

Sakamir was afraid of – the survivor of the original mission – the one she had planned to tame and force to reveal the secrets of the Soterion. Cyrus.

As she looked, she became aware of the moon behind him. Lower now, and its bright silver dulled to deep yellow, it hung over his head like a glow. She had seen the image before, many, many times. It was painted on the wall of her residence in Filna. Far away from there, amid fire and bloodshed, she was face to face with the pale dumbman in a yellow hat.

A troop of Kogon warriors, headed by Jinsha, was running up the slope towards Cyrus. Their spears were raised, ready to strike. If he didn't move fast, Xsani realised, they would kill him.

"Stop!" she commanded. "Leave him!"

Startled by the sudden cry, Cyrus glanced briefly towards her, spun round and vanished like smoke into the shadows.

Later, when Jinsha asked why she had saved that particular dumbman, the Malika was unusually reticent. All she would say was that he was needed.

"So everything's lost," said Miouda when Cyrus explained how he reached the Ghasar after the fire had started.

"Suppose so," he shrugged, struggling to prevent despair getting the better of him. "But we're still here. We'll get out, find another group of Constants and start again."

Aware how lame he sounded, he took Miouda in his arms and held her tight against his chest. "I'm sorry," he said quietly. "I'm so, so sorry."

She was too upset to reply. Overwhelmed by the utter

bleakness of their situation, she broke into uncontrollable sobs.

"Come on, you two," said Sammy after a short interval. "Yes, it's horrible, really horrible. And I've lost my Corby. But it could be worse, you know."

Cyrus looked at him. "Oh yes?"

"Yes! Listen, I've got a little surprise for you."

When they were bringing the books and the laptops up from the Soterion cave, he confessed, he had acted a bit deceitfully. He didn't like the idea of moving absolutely everything to Alba – just in case. When no one was looking, he had hidden something in a corner of the vault.

What? Cyrus asked.

A laptop. And what's more, it was a laptop with SP written on it, like that in the Ghasar. With a bit of luck, the one in the vault would also hold details of the Salvation Project.

Cyrus sighed. It was all very well, but did Sammy fancy going into Alba and searching for a key among hundreds of murderous Zeds?

The young man put his hand in the leather pouch at his side and brought out the object he had found hidden in the cushion.

"Guess what? It's the key to the vault! Nicked it from the Emiron when I called in. Sammy's got it sorted, see? So let's get out of here before them Zeds come looking for us."

Miouda turned to take one last look at the settlement that had been her home. "Oh look!" she exclaimed. "The fire! It's spreading."

Sparks from the blazing Ghasar had landed on thatched roofs nearby, setting them alight. The flames were spreading fast, carried by the light wind that had sprung up. Before long, the conflagration would engulf the entire settlement.

"Troy," muttered Cyrus as he gazed upon the dreadful scene. "It's Troy all over again!"

Cyrus, Miouda and Sammy, the only Constant survivors of the massacre of Alba, headed for the Soterion Gate in silence. The enormity of what they had witnessed and what was still going on around them made conversation impossible. There was so much to say but so little that could be expressed in words.

Keeping to the shadows, they avoided all contact with Zeds until they reached the gate itself. There they met with a very strange experience. Slipping through the arched doorway, they ran into a posse of four Zeds. Three of the men appeared to be guarding the fourth, a tall young man holding a vertical spear. Stuck on the spike at the top was a round, black object, rather like a giant fungus.

On seeing the Constants, the three Zed guards wanted to attack. The spear-carrier forbade it. "Ratbrains!" he shouted in an unearthly, high-pitched scream. "Would you leave your Over-Malik undefended as he enters the scene of his finest triumph? If you move so much as one batshit toe, vermin, I'll see you spitted and roasted like the pigs you are!"

The three Zeds trembled and stayed where they were, allowing the Constants to pass by unchallenged. When they looked back, the strange quartet had passed under the archway and was making its way along the street towards the square. "Bow!" the spear-carrier was screaming. "Bow before the

Mighty Timur!"

Sammy turned to Cyrus. "Is that what I think it was?"

"Yes. Didn't look much like him though, did it? But you heard what the man carrying him said. That was Timur alright."

"And good riddance," muttered Sammy, turning to the path that led to the Soterion.

The level ground around the entrance to the vault was quiet and peaceful. While Sammy went in to collect the hidden computer, Cyrus stayed outside with Miouda. The pair had hardly spoken to each other since leaving Alba.

She broke the silence. "There is hope, Cyrus," she said softly, putting her hand in his.

"I suppose so. If we can find some electricity. And if the laptop works."

"Yes. But there's more than that. Remember how I didn't want to jump off the wall?"

"Yes. Why was it?"

"Can't you guess?" She took his hand and placed it over her stomach. "I'm expecting a baby, Cyrus. Our baby."

A thousand emotions swept through him. "Oh Miouda! The best of times comes at the worst of times!"

She's right, he thought. There is always hope. There must be. And her pregnancy was a sign. Despite all the terrible suffering, cruelty and barbarity, they had to go on.

He heard the click of the lock as Sammy shut the Soterion door behind him. "Got it!" he called quietly as he hurried over to them. "Look!" He held out the laptop. "Untouched."

"The Long Dead would have called you a genius," Cyrus

smiled. Keeping one hand round Miouda's waist, he put the other on Sammy's shoulder. "Do you realise you have the past and future of humanity in your hands?"

"Not just in my hands, Cyrus. There's a little bit inside Miouda, too."

"You know?"

"She told me while you were down at the Ghasar. You'd still be with her, she said, even though you might not come back." He paused. "Anyway, I had an idea when she didn't want to jump off that wall."

"You're incorrigible, Sammy!" Cyrus said, still with his hand on the young man's shoulder. "Come on. Let's get as much distance as we can between us and those Zeds."

Thus – half in hope, half in fear – the three survivors set off into the wilderness. Like figures in a dance of the Long Dead, they walked abreast. The taller man in the middle had his arms affectionately round the shoulders of the other two, a young woman on his right and a young man on his left. Behind them, the sky blazed like a furnace. By sunhigh, when they finally lay down to rest, the place they had left was no more than blackened stones over which the ashes of the Soterion flickered like butterflies in the warm morning breeze.

Glossary

Alba   Constant settlement where the Soterion was found.

bodyburn   Constant term for cremation.

breeding slave Male Zed term for a woman kept to produce children.

Captain   Male Zed officer under the rank of Malik.

Constants   Those trying to maintain the civilisation that collapsed following the Great Death of 2018-19.

copemate   Alban name for a partner of either sex.

Death Month   28-day period during a person's 19th year when they age and die.

Della Tallis   Constant settlement where Cyrus was born and raised.

dumbman   Female Zed term for a male.

Emir   Elected leader of a Constant settlement.

Emiron   Emir's residence in Alba.

Eyes   Kogon lookouts and spies.

Filna   Abandoned Long Dead town inhabited by the Kogon.

flabtoad   Grozny term for a female.

Ghasar   Meeting place of Alba's Majlis.

Gova   Constant term for a mysterious power (electricity) worshipped by the Children of Gova.

Great Death	Period (2018–19) when all those over 19 suddenly aged and died.
Grozny	Tribe of vicious Zeds once led by Timur.
Gurkov	Zed tribe led by Ogg.
halfmoon	Constant term for a fortnight.
handshow	Constant term for a vote.
Kogon	Tribe of female Zeds.
Konnel	Alban officer.
kumfort	Kogon term for a partner, female.
Long Dead	Those whose civilisation died out during the Great Death.
Majlis	Constant council advising the Emir.
Malik	Male Zed tribal leader.
Malika	Female Zed tribal leader.
moon	Constant term for a month.
Over-Malik	Title given to Timur after his death.
spitfest	Grozny feast of spit-roasted meat, sometimes human.
sunhigh	Constant term for noon and South.
Tallin	Constant from Della Tallis.
wedun	Tallin term for a partner of either sex.
winter	Constant term for a year.
Zeds	Barbarians who reject the civilisation that collapsed during the Great Death.
Zektiv	Officer of the Kogon Zeds.

THE  MISSION

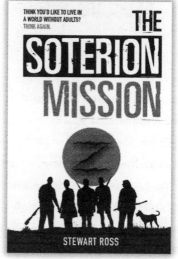

THINK YOU'D LIKE TO LIVE IN
A WORLD WITHOUT ADULTS?
THINK AGAIN.

THE SOTERION MISSION

STEWART ROSS

It is the year 2016 and all the adults are dead.

A horrific mutation in human DNA has resulted in a world of
children and adolescents, struggling to survive with no science,
art or learning of any kind. Each has only nineteen years to live:
nineteen years in which to be born, grow up, grow old and die.

Legend has it that the mysterious Soterion holds the key to
centuries of lost knowledge. The loyal Constants Roxanne
and Cyrus lead a mission to find the Soterion. On the way,
they must do battle with wild Zeds and outwit the false god
of the Children of Gova. But suspicion and jealousy threaten to
tear the mission apart. Will they learn to trust each
other before their time runs out?

About the author

Prizewinning author Stewart Ross taught at all levels in the UK, the USA, the Middle East and Sri Lanka before becoming a full-time writer. He has published many works, including novels for adults and for children. He has also written plays, lyrics and poetry, and his books have been translated into several languages. As a change from the large garden hut in which he works, Stewart ventures forth to schools, colleges and universities in the UK, France and elsewhere to talk about writing and pass on his passion for words.

For more exciting books from
brilliant authors, follow the fox!

www.curious-fox.com